The Oath

By G.R Coldicott

The Oath

Copyright © 2025 G.R Coldicott / Iron Realist Press

All rights reserved. No part of this book may be reproduced, stored in a retrieval system, or transmitted in any form or by any means—electronic, mechanical, photocopy, recording, or otherwise—without prior written permission of the author.

First Edition, 2025
ISBN: 9798298198592

Cover design: G.R Coldicott
Published by: Iron Realist Press

For those who stand, even when the tide turns.

The Hunt, 1062

The Earl stoops over a map. It is early morning in Winchester and the sun is barely winking. The large map, held fast on the table by candlesticks and sundry ornaments is stitched together vellum, scraped and smoothed by a monk's hand. He is on the ground floor and the hazy light in the roughly finished room hung with tapestries in the French style. He can read, like most of the English lords, even some Latin, speak enough French to exchange pleasantries. He has in mind something bold and secret; a Viking boldness that could gain his lord the upper hand without much bloodshed. The clumsy handle of the oak door startles him as the king slopes in.

"Harold," says Edward in his rich French accent.

"Yes, Lord," The Earl turns and bows his head slightly, giving a courteous half meeting of his eyes to his King's.

"Are you busy, Harold?"

"Busy, Lord?"

"Scheming, Harold. Not like your father of course?"

"No, Lord, planning for you. A raid," he was quick to respond. Edward's suspicion could turn on a penny into an outright inquisition.

"You aim to go Viking? Isn't that beneath you."

"In this case, Lord, no."

"You do love the sea, Harold."

"I get that from both my grandfathers, Lord."

"Yes, of course. Harold."

"Lord."

"It looks to be a fine morning."

"Lord."

"It is early yet."

"Yes, lord."

"I though perhaps, given the day, it seems likely to be that we could go out."

The earl looks up and gives his king a look. "Out, Lord?"

"Yes Harold. Go on and get that hawk of yours."

"Lord."

"Excellent, Harold. We see eye to eye."

Harold grins as the beaming king strides off down the hall, his tall frame scattering servants as he gives excited orders. The earl takes a last look at his map, sighs and goes for his gear.

The morning is fine, as the King had said. The whole court is now up and running around. Such is Edward, a man of each moment. Housecarls lazily strap on bracers and bark for the farriers to get their horses ready. Handlers soothe their hounds who are circling and whining. Edward's falconers hustle, their charges hooded and beaks wrapped shut. It is as if the town is under attack, such is the commotion. Servants gather spears and bows as the men of the court strap on their sidearms and yawn into the forecourt.

Tostig and Gyrth come out together, tall like their brother, dressed in similar red tunics and blue leggings, clumsily pulling their boots up. The Queen, their sister, barely made up and blinking, follows behind from her rude awakening. Aelfgar, Earl of Mercia, has caught up with Harold, who, unusually, is carrying his own bird, a goshawk, its orange eye as yet uncovered. He is pestering Harold about upcoming action against the Welsh. Harold is mute. Stigand strides through, more an earl than a man of the cloth, strapping on his dagger and smiling at the scene.

'Harold," he booms. "Are you responsible for this?"

"I'm just following along like the rest of you." He is grateful for the reprieve from Aelfgar. "Say, bishop, have you a new diocese?"

"New Diocese, since when?"

"Last night, perhaps." quips Harold and nudges Aelfgar, who scowls.

Harold calls for his eldest. He calls again. The boy, turned fourteen, scampers out, dishevelled and panicked. The men gathered laugh.

"Come, boy. It's time to hunt. Edmund too. Fetch him and find a palfrey."

Here comes Edith fair and foul mouthed, her gaggle around her.

"I'm staying with mother," she says. No arguing. Gytha so sturdy, tall. Up and about already, managing her household; always busy, busy. Giving orders to his household. He nods and moves to kiss her. She meets his lips. Still so fair, this Edith. Still so warm.

"Taking the boys?"

"Just the two." Magnus, too young, glares at his father and stomps off past his mother. No arguing. His time will come.

Harold calls for his horse and hauls himself up. He raises a hand to his wife – she nods and guides the remaining children back into the shadows of the palace.

The chaos grows and envelops the town, before receding into an orderly trot and trudge out of the great gate of Winchester and into the fields beyond. The great, nimble, mass of the court spreads out through the open fields, ceorls and slaves alike pausing in their morning's chores to look on at these men of leisure. Everyone smiles and waves to Harold with his ready laugh and goshawk perched on his outstretched hand, like some holy processional gesture. The boys riding beside him ready for trouble. Only his housecarls call him "Lord." The morning dew licks the feet of horses and men as they sweep over the green fields of Hampshire where its great Earl held dominion, right at the gates of the capital. The Earl glances at Edward, the King laughing heartily with Gyrth and Stigand, that wily collector of offices, filling the whole gathering with the same enthusiasm. Around him too, the remnant Normans with their poor English and worse manners, plotting always to secure the succession.

He looks at his sons, eyes narrowing in mock suspicion. Harold and his five brothers played in these fields as boys; fought and raced, hunted and thieved, so much so that he was almost as much of the soil and the sea as the ceorls that farmed the land and answered his call. Raised between the court and the fields – and the ships his father had sent him to learn and lead, Wessex is to him as it was to the average man who tilled the soil: the earthy root of his life. He wonders at these two, what small crimes they had committed under the English sun.

As far as the eye could see, and beyond, is Harold's. And it is not. The hides folded into the hundreds into the shires and the counties into the Earldom but each man owns his share. Wessex. Held by duty, bound by oaths, tied to men who could vanish into the soil like mist under sun. As his father had learned all those years ago, the Fyrd, the folk, could drag their heels and leave a lord stranded; as the tides turn, so the Fyrd. Harold gives a ready grin to everyone who meets his gaze. Aside from a scattered assortment of servants, there are few French among the crowd. All tolerated the sweetmeats and preparations Edward favoured, so long as the influence ended there. Godwin had won. Harold had prospered. Behind him Gyrth and Tostig with the broad Stigand rolling on his horse and Leofwyn, hustling to catch up with Harold, long haired and wild.

"Are we on then, Harold?" In his late twenties, Leofwyn is charged with assisting in the Godwins' business assets. No real land or title, and a young wife pregnant again. Harold pauses.

He nods and turns to his bird. Words are few between them since their exile in Ireland. A look, a gesture is enough. Far from their father and the rest of the tribe, Harold taught him the sea and the raid, how to manage a formation, clear a deck, and lead men. And trade. He couldn't get the boy to sit still, but he made a devoted companion of him. Loyal.

They are headed South, towards the downs. There is forest there as well as the wide expanse of chalky hills perfect for falconry. The horde is careful not to trample the fields, ready for planting this spring, keeping to the fallow land and the trackways. Now and then Harold bellows at a servant, a thegn, an earl – even the Queen to keep off. Only the King will be spared his tongue if he strays onto precious soil or property.

"Edith, keep your people off the fucking farmland," he bellows.

"Oh!" The Queen, still groggy from her rude awakening; "Ladies, keep off will you, there's good people." Poor Edith, or perhaps happy woman, spared the gropings of a fat lord, in her marriage to the chaste Edward. Chaste…although who knows what went on? Perhaps only Edith. Perhaps only those French the king kept on. Rife with gossip, this court. He had sworn an oath when Godwin forced her on him, not to touch her as a man a woman, yet he seems not to touch anyone. She looks to Harold for approval, her innocent eyes so disarming, but he scowls at his older sister and kicks his heel into his dark destrier. Schemer.

South-east from Winchester lies Bosham – seaport and his second home – the place he learned the sea and its tempers. From where he sailed to take on Baldwin. Twenty-Seven and given his father's nod. Perhaps he would visit after. Take a ship and sail around to Bristol with Leofwyn. See how business is, get news of Wales, finalize the plan. A raid on a place he had never seen. Viking. Harold Halfdane grins and turns his horse to his brothers.

Tostig, almost handsome, with almost delicate features, but a grim turn around the mouth, a trimmed moustache and finely barbered strap around his chin. Touching the gilded cross he wore outside of his tunic out of habit; piety, or show of it. Harold and he a year apart, rivals, that year a gulf between them, their status. He, the accidental pater familias, the second son, the one to risk, Tostig, just a year off. Harold in Flanders, Tostig at home, pious, waiting. Like a serpent? Gyrth alongside him, the joker, like Harold. Broad faced and laughing Gyrth. Leaner and pensive Tostig.

"Brothers, good morning," says the great Earl. Gyrth gives a twinned grin with Harold; Tostig merely smiles and nods a humble greeting.

"How's that hawk of yours, and how is your arm not falling off?" Gyrth admires the bird as its head flits back and forth and those primal yellow eyes blink.

"He seems to like it with me – hates the falconers at court for some reason. Always flustered and pecking at them."

"Strange bird."

"True, but bold and deadly. And loyal."

"When is Leofwyn going to be an Earl, Harold?" Gyrth laughs as Tostig scowls and buries his chin. Aelfgar, father-in-law to the Welsh king, trots politely besides the brothers "I hear Mercia will have an opening soon," Gyrth turns to face Aelfgar with a grin. Edwin, Aelfgar's eldest, shifts uncomfortably in his saddle.

"Over my dead body," the Earl says.

"Yes," says Harold, "that exactly." And the men around laugh along, all except Aelfgar and his sons. Harold seeks out the king with his keen eyes; the King, overhearing, smiles. All is well, still. "You there! Get the fuck off of that enclosure!"

"Stupid bitch!" A farmer's wife yells. Yes, that exactly.

The servants start to gain ground now, hurrying ahead. Ladies and men rudely shoved by the movement of carts and horses, whipped along. The housecarls of the various Earls fan out ahead even of them, their thick leather jerkins a contrast to the bright coloured tunics of their lords. Watchful, minding the path out of habitual care for their paymasters. Edward's men stay close to him, a shield even against the Queen. England, land of the free. Of the murderous knife.

At last, under the great broad sky lit up now, the sun dappling through the cirrocumuli and the downs just ahead, the host approach their meeting point. By this time, the servants have set up pavilions and began the process of making fires and boiling water. Wine and ale are laid out on tables offloaded from carts. Men carrying loads upon their bent backs. Offloading and setting up the mobile court. The housecarls form a perimeter around the camp while some sallied out to monitor the downs.

*　　*　　*

Out on the Downs, Harold and the King sit quietly on their horses, Tostig close by and watchful.

"Look, there, Harold. See my bird."

The falcon wheels in the pale blue sky and snatched at a small bird in flight.

"Outstanding!" The King cries. Off in the distance, hounds barked and men cried out. "Where is your oddity? Taken off, has he?"

Harold nods over to their left, His Goshawk swooping towards the ground, rises almost at the last moment clutching a young rabbit. The assembled group gasps and applauds.

"Well Harold. Your bird's bold to upstage the King's." The king laughs and touches his Earl's arm. "Harold."

"Yes Lord."

"I hate you less than your father."

"Well, that's a ringing fucking endorsement," laughs Stigand, seated nearby on his horse with the rest of the nobles, clapping his hands in delight.

"Lord."

"Much less, Harold." The King smiles gently at him.

"Stag!" The cry went up.

"Spear!. You there – fetch me a spear." The king grasps the hastily offered spear and takes off towards the sound of the braying hounds. Tostig follows close behind with Girth and the other lords. Harold waits for his bird to deposit its prey and nods to his handler to bind and hood it. He lets out a long breath through his lips before heading at a canter behind the excited host.

As the afternoon wears on the King and his entourage settle into their camp. The nearby folk trickle in from their towns and farmsteads bringing vegetables and bread to the feast. All mill about, talking with servants and lords alike, cuffing the boys' heads, heedless of the housecarls around the king. And so the king holds court with his people, and grievances and needs are shared with the Earl, who takes note and shares his meal with his folk. Fresh meat and ale. Life itself.

*   *   *

At first light, after a night in their tents, Harold and Leofwyn set out with thirty men. Taking leave of the king, he has a messenger ride to Alfred, his chief, in Winchester. Sending the boys, slumped on their horses after a night of ale, back to his wife with a bodyguard, the earl rides down towards Bosham. Locals and servants greet him with nods and salutations as he carries on. He rests a while at his hall, and has a thrall wash his hair and groom him before he takes to ship at the jetty. He takes eight capable sailors stationed in the barracks by his snekkja, The Worm, a ship of twenty-four oars. Three such ships are moored here and twelve at Southampton. Off in the distance two ships from his coast guard patrol between her and Southampton. He will see to that town on the return. Leofwyn roughly shunts the helmsman off from his place. "Mine," he says. A thegn at the rudder. What a sight. Warriors settle into their places at the oars as men on shore push the boat off from the pier. Water laps against the hull. All is well.

The men begin to row at an easy pace until they clear the nearshore tides, Leofwyn hits the tiller and yells to the crew, their backs to portside, the starboard crew heaving backwards. Once aligned by the land across from the Solent, the sail is lowered and the oars pulled up. To the left across the Solent the Isle of Wight with its white cliffs and low beaches marks the end of Harold's domain. They hug the coast through the narrow straights under a cool bright spring sun. The thirty men sing in English, then Danish, to the beat of a drum, Harold leaning at the prow with its Wyvern figurehead. Wessex. Within a few short hours they are past Southampton and at the arc of sand of Bournemouth and by early afternoon reach the sandbanks. The route is crowded with fishing vessels and the occasional merchant ship. Harold motions to Leofwyn to let them pass, his hair swept back and forth by the sea breeze, his eyes bright. The sail is raised and the men take to their oars, waiting for an opening. Slipping through the entrance to Poole Harbor. Keen eyed men on land hunt for a friendly sign and see the prow, Harold raises an arm and the ship proceeds past Brownsea Island and finally up to the mouth of the Frome, where they drop anchor by a jetty. Here the men can rest, under strict orders, while their Lord proceeds with his brother and six men to the Reeve.

"Lord, why do we always moor so far from the town," Olaf, one of his Danish Carls tramps unhappily with his Dane axe slung over one shoulder.

"Free flow of commerce," Leofwyn drones like a rote student.

Harold nods. Olaf is keenly looking for horses to requisition; Harold smirks. The other men follow their lord without outward complaint. This will be a drawn-out trip. They all know he's up to something but the ports are full of ears and mouths. The day is spent visiting with leading men and merchants. The Reeve, a large man known for his strength, grips Harold's great arm like a brother.

They'll take turns lifting stones tonight; shouldering, carrying. The younger brother busies himself around town, through the grid and the stinking streets, taking stock of trade and the kinds of men in town. Tallying and watching, exchanging greetings, natural as Harold now. Ranulph, the Reeve presents a list of criminal acts to Harold, who agrees to stay an extra day to preside over the shire court. From theft to arson, death in a fair fight to a backstabbing. Justice must be done. The wergild must be paid. A thegn too has to pay. Even a thrall is worth something to their master. The crew are summoned. They can stay the night.

Harold and the strong men of the town compete at the stones. Each man braces his back and wraps his arms around a large stone, too awkward for most men to carry. Then they heave it up and carry their burden as far as their bodies permit. A crowd gathers, but no one bets against their lord. The Reeve wins in the carry, but only by a short yard. Harold takes the largest stone. Leofwyn laughs off a challenge and reclines with the men. Only Olaf rises to the bait and almost meets his master in strength. They drink, eat and listen to the people. Tomorrow, justice. Then they carry on.

Harold sits in the meeting hall. The jury are seated around him on stools and sacks. He listens attentively, always making eye contact under the fringe of hair that falls about his forehead. Eyes that meet and travel down. Here he stops a thegn from biased questions and queries a shifty eyed oath-helper, his half-raised hand enough to quell a storm. No death results from this day, just the wergild and the cost of time.

* * *

There is no shortcut to Bristol. Not only because the river passages require portage of a boat, which is slow and takes men away from their duties. The men are used to detours and all the obligations that distract them from their destination. It is mid-afternoon; they are putting in at Weymouth for the evening, to make some time at least. There, they stay the night on the boat, eating at a poor inn. The next day, stiff from the rough sleeping they take to sea and make a straight line to Exmouth. It is raining a lightly on the men who wait at the mouth of the Ex for a navigator. He takes them halfway to a mooring spot where they disembark for a barge. This time they do not walk and the whole crew departs. The ship is safe here. Up the river, the long barges and small craft painted in dull shades reds and blacks bustle past carrying their bales of wool and skins out to sea, loaded with cloth, or fish on the return. Harold hails each boat as he can, some in awe, some as familiar as old friends. Always 'Harold'. Up to the great stone walls of Exeter built before English memory. At a stable, Harold and his men take to horse and amble through the great gate studded with iron. The large town carries its waste through the streets; no need to muck it out. He heads to the Bishop's home, through the narrow streets, timber buildings looming. The stench and noise. where Aelfgar held court. Both the local and the Shire Reeve of Devon will be summoned. Aethelmar a prominent thegn in Devon was visiting with Aelfgar – there was no time or reason to call the rest of the notable men. He could pay visits later.

"We have an outlaw problem," says Aelfgar, thick and sturdy and dressed in a finely spun woollen tunic.

"Punishments are too expensive, taxes are too high," the local Reeve says. The Shire Reeve shakes his head.

"It's peace that's the problem. Fighting men with too much time on their hands."

"Farmers are fighting men, fisherman too," says Harold, then, nodding to his bodyguard "These men live only by their sword – they don't cause trouble in peace."

Aelfgar snorts. Housecarls were notorious for their nighttime revelries.

"It's the Wergild," the local Reeve says. Believable, but then what consequence for manslaughter?

"I have thirty men," the earl says, "Give me thirty more. From your guard, too Aelfgar. I need a ship too, for later. We're headed to Bristol on business, and I need an extra ship for safety." Wales is close — a few small craft set around his ship could easily cause him trouble.

"A ship will be no issue lord; we have crews ready too from the coast guard." This Reeve is organized. Harold will check the books soon, take his share, and the King's.

As the meeting closes, the Archbishop, stout and warlike, sits back and strokes his beard. "Earl Harold, might we talk in private? The succession."

The others file out, and Leofwyn closes the door slowly behind him, hearing only "About the boy Edgar."

After a morning immersed in ledgers and profit, Harold claps the Reeve on the shoulder. A good choice this man. Gold will be sent under guard to Winchester along with fine cloth. Men are sent back with thralls for armour and weapons. The Shire Reeve assembles his twenty-five men and the Bishop loans ten good housecarls. That's sixty, with Harold, Leofwyn, and the Reeve. As evening closes, they head out of the city fast and hard on horseback. A sighting around Haldon Forest; hopefully they could catch a few. Make an example. The common law did not apply to these men.

Catching the first man is easy. They leave their horses with a guard and make their way at an acute angle from the usual vantage points. Past the oaks and ash trees. Quickly, quiet as burglars. At failing light Bjorn, a Danish housecarl, lets loose an arrow at a man as he looks the wrong way down a slope. His cry sends others scattering. These men are clumsy – not hardened criminals. Desperate. They catch a few in the semi-circle they had set up above the overlook after hiking through the dense woods. Two of the Bishop's men with their throats slit, caught out. And the Reeve bloodied from a live one who kicked out. Five. A good catch. They take them to their lookout, aware of the eyes around them in the forest, on the cliffs.

"My lord, I killed a man in a fair fight – the wergild, it was too much for me to pay so I was outlawed."

"Lord, they came for taxes when I lost half my sheep. What am I to do when they make me a nihling for poverty?" Something more in this man's eyes – some other act following the forfeiture.

So they were banished, took to thieving and murdering. Better to have done it in another man's land, not close to home. Not to their own.

Harold nods, hears their quavering voices and their pleas. Just as the town Reeve said. There will be change, or Devon will be infested with their kind. He hangs them from branches on the overlook and gives his men orders to gather their own dead.

"We were nihlings once," says Leofwyn quietly as they ride back to town.

"Yes," his brother looks at him with that half gaze as they trot back to the city walls, "It came to mind."

At Exeter Harold assembles his men. They are choosing from known men among the housecarls and sailors here. None with connections to Bristol, all loyal and hardened. There would be three ships total. Ninety to one hundred men. Enough. Leofwyn and

Raedwulf, a lean man of thirty-five, share the commands with him. They will allocate their own men after he takes the first crop. Protection from pirates for the Earl. Harold arranges payment to the families of the dead housecarls. He takes leave of the city Reeve with a firm handshake. Regular patrols will be sent out to mind for outlaws, and he gives instructions to lower the wergild. Fisherman and merchants move around them, occasionally having a gawp at their Earl.

"Take care to mind a man's situation when collecting taxes – we don't want an army of the disaffected hounding the countryside. You're a fine Reeve, keep the lines of communication open and carry on." The earl, dressed in a fresh green tunic of finely spun wool, neatly shaved and his moustache and hair groomed, moves off to his ship. The crew heave off and row out into the Exmouth towards the dark blue sea. The Reeve is full of pride as he waves them off.

On to Watchet, the sky slightly threatening, Harold at the stern gazing occasionally over to his brother and Raedwulf's ships strung out behind. Gulls wheel into shore and back again. He'll keep watch on the clouds and the moisture in the air. Looking at the men, every face familiar, every name and quirk. Danes, Englishmen and a rare Norwegian like Olaf. Most taller than other men, able to sweep and swing and hook their axes in the second rank of a shield wall.

There are Asbjorn & Bjorn – brothers who signed on at the same time, from the Danelaw – an excellent team in a shield wall or deck.

Eadric, scarred and gnarled like an oak, still hard at forty.

Wulfstan from Bristol – used to border raids and tough as iron.

Wynstan, from Southampton – trained by Carls who took pity on a sailor's orphan.

Edward, youngest son of a thegn – fled the monastic life and pledged to his Earl.

Edwin, monkish looking and utterly profane; excellent with a sword.

Hereward, an Englishman from the North, cunning, ruthless.

Cyneweard – ruddy as the farmer he was – picked up by Harold for bravery in the field.

Harald the Dane, stocky and middling height, able to see a gap and plug or breach it.

Ivar, half stooped and shifty like the thief he was as a boy.

Leif, exiled from Denmark for an honour killing; savage in battle.

Olaf, large and brawny, always questioning, rarely satisfied; huge and devastating in a charge.

Ragnald with his loping gait and miserly look.

Sigurd, thin and sickly looking but excellent on an axe.

Sven, tall and lean with a thick scar down his face, worth two men at an oar or when clearing a deck.

Thorkel, whose father was a Varangian, tall with a fine flowing moustache.

Ulf with his ready smile and jokes, a favourite, capable, not outstanding but dependable.

Valdemar, finely groomed and meticulous in his work.

Aethelred the ready, watchful as a shepherd.

Aethelstan, rough and ready despite his birth, quick to a quip and anger.

Beornwulf, a man seemingly running to fat but fast and accurate with his Dane axe.

Ceolwulf, scowling and broken in his heart; some woman perhaps. Vicious.

Erik from Norway, clumsy with his words and the butt of jokes.

Halfdan, like Harold, easily passing between the tribes of men.

Aelfgar, hair cropped short with a large beard, fierce and wild as the Irish.

Dunstan, balding and red faced, as if always angry, but a happy man, careful to please his lord.

Oswald, handsome and charming, one for the ladies and trusted with secrets – a good agent for diplomacy and intrigue.

Wulfric, dark haired, sly, stealthy and utterly ruthless – his main scout and a confident in strategy; while he held no rank above the others, they all knew his place in the lord's favour. He is key to the plan.

All here with him share the camaraderie of men who fight and sleep together, shit in the same bucket.

* * *

At Watchet he sits with the Reeve and the merchants and discusses the wool trade. Unlike Exeter, the simple timber buildings and wooden jetties subject to the ravages and repairs of raids and time the simple port town seemed a scarecrow against the large, variegated cliffs. But it bustles with activity – the land around is perfect for grazing and the market is packed with wool. It is shearing season – critical months in the English trade with Flanders and Normandy. Farmers and merchants alike in dull tunics but bright smiles. Harold assembles the town merchants and Reeve to discuss town improvements. They are unanimous – the Earl or the King must pay.

"In that case," their lord says, "I'll have to raise the taxes." He smiled at their collective scowls. "Then again, if I tax finespun cloth, all you fancy men will walk around in homespun rags. And if I tax your rags…"

And so it goes; he would have to fork out without a repeat of the issues in Exeter. Spring and Autumn are fat times for these men, but the intervening months and winters are hard.

"Reeve, I'll give you three months to cost out improvements and present your plan to me at Winchester."

"I'll need four, lord. The accounting and the sowing are taking up my time now, I'll not have anything to show except barebones." Harold nods, at least the man has an inkling of the task ahead.

They go for a meal of lamb at the hall, the great door creaking in the breeze and occasional drops of water falling upon them from the old roof. Next, he greets the farmers and walks around the market asking after business and the odd familiar wife. Sitting at the Reeve's rough table, coin and woolsacks strewn around him under a low timber and daub ceiling with, Harold tuts at the accounting. Motioning to his brother they step out of the Reeve's hall and have some horses bridled. Out on the moor for a short ride to ease the monotony of sea travel.

"I'll give him five months and then get Edwin, thegn, to find a replacement," he says to Leofwyn. "Just the two of us out, like old times." They smile to each other.

"Good place for hawking, this," notes his brother as they scan the heathered hills and wide moorland.

"Now why didn't I think of that?"

"Always rushing out, Harold." Harold strokes his long blond moustaches, stretching across his handsome face, and nods.

With the sun just arcing towards the horizon, they turn their mares back and meet up with their men.

As they head towards the ship, the local priest, lean and pious in his brown habit, comes up to give a blessing.

"I think you mean Tostig," says Leofwyn smiling. The priest gives a confused shake of his head.

"I'll take all the blessings I can get," says Harold, as he bows his head slightly.

* * *

Again, into the deep channel, round the toe of England and the old jagged British ruins cropping up on the cliffs. The men of Cornwall with their strange tongue. Best left to themselves and a gentle yoke. Here the waters are calm again and the wind is with them, the sun strays across the sky and the men idle in the ship. They've been waiting since late morning. The sun crawls into its zenith and they resume, rowing with the flood tide. On to Portishead where they pick up a pilot who, timing the tides, takes them the last few miles up the Avon, the craggy gorges framing the river as the three ships ease into port. They moor against a well-maintained jetty.

The hustle of merchants and sailors. Stench of cargo. Men make way as naturally as water as the great ones disembark and move along. Nods, and the occasional neck bow as Harold progresses. Past the ditch and through the stone gatehouse they move, the whole crew heading to the hall where Alfred waits. Wales is close. Time for tight lips and open trade.

Assembled before them are five crews of men; a third of his household. These were the most seaworthy of the finest men in English war making. Not a nervous twitch among the group, not a questioning look. Direct gazes and uncompromising loyalty. Dark men and fair, tall and hard as timbers. Alfred, chief of his guard, stands, his thick forearms wide as legs, and a long moustache stretching down his broad cheeks, surveying the men.

"Our trade with Ireland has been impacted by piracy, as is common knowledge. We will accompany a fleet of ships to Dublin and organize a coast guard with our Irish partners." So far so good. "As necessary we will strike those ports that support piracy."

The gathered host seem to lean back with interest.

"Yes, you'll get a fight or two." The men laugh. "Anyone from Wales among us?"

Noone moves, save after a beat, a tall blond Carl raises his hand.

"Bjorn, you're a Dane," the broad and fierce Alfred laughs. He nods his head up and down with an idiot grin.

"Wulfric, aren't you half Welsh?" Wulfric scowls and Harold motions the crews to silence.

"An unavoidable, and unfortunate heritage, certainly."

"My mother's side," the dark and wily Wulfric says.

"Hereward, you're dark," smiles Harold.

"My hair is brown, lord."

"Looks like one of them anyway," Olaf laughs. "Throw him on shit heap for a while and he'll be just the right colour." Hereward gives a half eye roll and purses his lips.

"Close enough, go take a walk with Wulfnoth."

"Lord."

"Mind those bears too," yells Bjorn and the men laugh.

The vast timber hall is theirs, much to the dismay of the Reeve, who has no warning for the victualing and sleeping arrangements. The whole town will be on edge. They'll let the story out soon enough.

"Men," roars Harold.

"Lord!" as one

"Keep your dicks in your breeches and your knives sheathed."

Silence.

"For now."

They roar.

Out they go to a man past the great walls and the ditch, out of Bristol already.

* * *

Housecarls splitting wood, hauling logs as a unit. Shields locking. Maintain the line. Men behind swing axes at ghosts. Close quarters work. Men carrying rocks forward and backward, heaving up and running with their loads. Men in mail dancing, jumping, leaping between points as if between decks. Men wrestling in the muck in full gear. Face the gauntlet. Swing the long axe in a sweeping line. Splitting wood. Hauling logs. Sweat and strain. The unit. Harold strips down. He trains with his men out in the green fields beyond Bristol. His brother close and laughing with the housecarls as they haul each other down. Soon, his sons, learning the drills forming into lines and filling the gaps. Three men in a shield wall to one man behind, archers between them. Packed tight they drill ten on ten, man against horseman and man against wall of men. Hook and pull. Clear the decks. Clean the fields. Hour upon hour they drill, not at sea, now on land. Forming and dispersing, storming a wall. Some men of the fyrd come up from Bristol, bearing their own shields and spears. A good time to train them in holding the line. Tricking and trapping, goading the boys until they stand firm as can be in the face of the enemy.

"Here is the wall lads," says Harold and hurls his great body at a group of interlocked shields. It holds. "Against a man, a horse, an army – the shield wall must hold." They know this, but it's a sight to see their Earl large and muscular in his breeches, gleaming and mighty, bruised and merry at the war play.

They take their turn, carls hooking their shields down, knocking their heads, finding a gap and pulling them down. Again and again until there's a crowd forming, and more of the townsmen come to take their turn. This is how armies are made, with these men carrying the wisdom with them to the fields and Fyrd-gatherings. Some here have seen action, against Welsh raids, or raided themselves, many not but the inspiration of the next few days may set them on the path. Laughter always, and the Earl's temper flaring and roaring back into laughter, each failure the spark.

"Right lad," Harold pulls a man down as if he's a child, "you're dead. You there: pull him back, that's right, drag him; stop struggling! You - fill the gap. Shove in and lock."

"How come I died," the man being dragged on his back whined

"That's war, love," laughed a Carl. "There's no rhyme or reason, you just fell."

"Then at last the brave warrior could no longer stand fast," sang Beornwulf, and the others nodded.

"But stand fast," says Harold flatly. The men laugh.

*   *   *

So the days go by, with training, administration, and the outfitting of ships. Six days in, Harold and Leofwyn sit like boys on a wall by the quay.

"Remember how desperate we were? Swein took off so fast he left his boat here."

"It was his third exile, I think. Edward gave us a lot of time to leave," Harold watches as the wretched cargo trudge, their hands bound in front, roped together. Women and children, the odd man, helpless and filthy. "He left that boat full of gold."

"Didn't he ask for it back?"

"What gold?" They grin.

"He wanted his land back from you too, I remember."

"He shouldn't have done what he did to Bjorn."

"I miss him." Harold nods; they pause and watch as a girl falls and her bound mother tries to help her up.

"As far as exiles go, it wasn't the worst situation."

"A full crew, treasure and Dublin." Yes, Dublin on Swein's coin. "Bishop Wulfstan wants this ended," pointing at the scene beyond them.

"Wulfstan gets his cut." They look away as the ship's master drags the girl up and shoves the mother forward.

"A beautiful morning, lords!" The ship's master raises his hand to the lords. Harold gives a half-raised hand and a smile. Leofwyn looks towards the sky; bright and cloudless. God's glory.

"The girls in Ireland," Harold shakes his head.

"They were something."

* * *

It's a small fleet - some twenty ships, mostly squat trading vessels with five of the earl's longships and a further two of the coast guard. Wulfric is back, Hereward quiet and attentive by his side. Nobody mentioned their absence; Wulfric was always coming and going. He confers with his lord and the longboat captains. Across the river into Wales and two days ride to meet their man. The news is good and the weather maintains its fairness; just the light rain so common here. The ships are loaded with supplies and armour, scaling ladders made of rope, ladders of wood, torches, axes, bows and spears. They will accompany the merchants to Dublin first, then find their targets as they come. The ships with their goods and human cargo are assembled to begin the perilous exit on the ebb tide. Each ship has its own navigator, the earl is bearing the cost and has his ship lead the way down the Avon to the estuary, great waves heaving them out to sea. Here and there a large swell, though the weather is still fair and the treacherous waves are absent this day. Wrecks of boats stranded and abandoned focus the mind. No ships are beached on the shallows and his captains signal to him as the fleet sets out into the Bristol channel. All is well.

They set out towards the Irish sea, the gulls and the waves in their strange dissonance dominating their ears. No hugging the shoreline – straight to Dublin. Towards the late afternoon, rounding Pembrokeshire, they spot three ships heading out towards them. They're fast boats, hardly a threat to any but a single merchant ship, which they tend to team up on. After a while they've seen enough and they head back to their cove. The hours pass under fair spring skies until the sun tips into the sea and they reduce sail overnight. Time to sleep in shifts; the moon is up so they have a clear enough view around them and the assigned watchmen have their bows ready at points around the ship.

"Fair winds for us, fair winds for pirates," notes Edward, trying to settle into a space between the benches.

"A more obvious truth has never been spoken," Wulfstan, a regular on sea voyages from Bristol as a boy, shakes his head.

"Get some sleep lads," their lord admonishes.

Morning comes after two watches and a false alarm. They eat a breakfast of cold bacon, hard boiled eggs and fresh bread, washed down with light ale. As the ships arc towards Dublin, Harold takes his horn and blows it twice. He nods to Ragnald at the helm and raises his hand to Wynstan and Leif at the sheets. They have the confused sailors adjust the sail as Ragnald leans towards starboard. The ship moves away from their small fleet. Only the two coast guard ships keep their course as Leofwyn orders his sail trimmed and slows. The other boats follow suit and Harold orders his crew to trim the sail too. The four longships form into a staggered line.

"Men."

They all look up towards their lord.

"I haven't been straight with you, but now there's no escaping we can talk freely." They all looked at their leader as if with one eye.

Across the water he knows Leofwyn and the other captains were having their talk.

"What is it Lord, another exile?" Laughed Olaf, the men all grin.

"It's a long way back to Bristol without a boat, Olaf. No, not exile." He paused.

"We're going to Rhuddlan to take the Welsh king. Dead or alive."

"Well, that's a fine way to die, lord," Thorkel laughed.

Off in distance they hear a loud cheer followed by another fainter one.

"That, Thorkel, is the reaction I was looking for." The men laugh and clap each other. They give a big cheer to save face with the other crews. Harold shakes his head with a smile.

"Just us, then lord?"

"All one hundred and fifty of us, yes. We will take the lead, Leofwyn and his men supporting the assault; Alfred will wait to storm after we get the gates open. One crew will remain to guard the ships. If we pull this off, we stop that bastard Gruffyd and his raids on Wessex." This time they did cheer.

"And we show up Aelfgar, Lord." Oh, that too, very much that.

"Hereward, Ragnald, Wulfstan, Leif – well done." Not a word from their lips. "Not that I don't trust all of you lads, but Bristol has a thousand Welsh ears." They all nod, the awe at their lord's audacity settling on them.

"This is going to be a great tale for the ages," shouts Olaf as a great wave slaps the men's faces.

Off on the slave ship, the captain looks over in alarm.

"Now where the fuck are they going?"

*   *   *

The ships head north, banking east as they pass Holy Island and Anglesey. At this rate they will hit the beaches at dusk. They keep on straight in case of watchers or stray boats that cross their path, before banking hard right. The captains have orders to gather at Harold's next horn blow if the seas were calm. As the sun leaned over to the west the ships slapped near to one another. There are cheers for Harold and Leofwyn, Alfred and the others were grinning over their crews.

"Are we sailing up the river, Harold," Alfred bellows across two other ships. Harold shakes his head; Gruffyd may be ready for them. Getting caught with archers either side of them and a river trap would be a pitiful way to go.

"We'll beach at nightfall, Edmund and his crew will stay behind with the ships – make sure you post archers and men to watch them at two hundred feet and more, the rest of us will make the trek to the fort on foot. My crew – leather jerkins and helmets only with rope ladders – Leofwyn – yours too. Leofwyn – you bank round the south as we come in from the North. Shields also and have a few men haul the Dane axes. Alfred, Edmund – your crews will come in armour to the West, where the main gate is. Wulfric will lead us to the king's chamber – Leofwyn will carry on sentry cleanup and get the gates open. The rest of you bide your time until we get Gruffydd. Then we take the king out the front gates with Alfred and crew as a rear guard."

"That's a plan," the scarred Edmund shouts with a laugh.

"If anything goes wrong – how could it – Alfred, you and your crews enter and raise hell. The rest of us will regroup with you."

"Liverpool is close by," how could Aelfgar object to them putting in for repairs? "Blackpool too – home. We can Sail to Northumbria in half a day if needed."

Alfred raises his arm. "Harold!"

The men shout their lord's name, banging their feet on the floor.

"Stealth, boys!" The men laugh and quiet down.

*   *   *

Evening comes and they hoist the sails. Time to row. They come close together and Harold lights a torch to guide the trailing ships. Wulfric is brought up to sight the landing place – a stony beach half a mile from the river mouth. The men have their bows and axes ready at their feet. Their long Norman shields will be left behind. Then darkness comes upon them. Off in the distance a lonely torch lights up and blinked four times. Wulfric nods and they row gently up to the shore, mindful of the noise. The ship beaches with a final heave and the crew pulled in their oars and gather their things. The sailors will stay with the ships. Harold first, then Wulfric and the others jump into the shallow water and run up to make a beachhead among the dank mists. Leofwyn comes up quickly behind and places his hand on his brother's back. The embers of a torch are just visible and Wulfric gives a quick whistle. It is returned. A man slips out of the gloom towards them and settles down. It's hard to make him out but he is the same build as Harold's man. They wait and watch as the other crews disembark. An old man, barely visible in the dark, potters across their field of view. Wulfric quick as can be darts out and brings the man down, dragging his still body back towards the beach.

"Off to a quick start there," the stranger whispers as Wulfric returns.

They head off behind this stranger, trusting in Wulfric's trust.

The way to the fort is straightforward, but they need to watch for people and soldiers patrolling. It's quiet and the half-moon just lights the way, stars strung low over the sky. Behind them, Alfred and his men a good hundred paces back clanking in their mail. Again, they stop – this time four men are laughing together in Welsh outside a squat hut near the riverbank. Harold motions to six of his men. They move forward, knives drawn and as one unit bring the poor men down as one, slitting their throats while the two warriors left swiftly enter the hut. Clear. They drag the bodies inside.

"We'll say a prayer for them later," Harold assures his men. He can't see, but knows they are grinning.

The keep on through the darkness and the mists, following their guide. Just off in the distance hazy lights smudge in the sky. They are upon the fort. Leofwyn comes up to Harold and they move with Wulfric and his man, keeping low and listening for voices. The great ditch surrounds the fort. There to the right of them, the gate, facing the river. The palisades, twice or more the height of a man are interspersed with watch towers; simple yet enough of an obstacle for an army. They watch for patrols; none outside the gates but men trudge with regularity on the walls, and sentries guard the towers.

"We need to be quick," says Leofwyn.

"Go left and take the east side," I'll take this approach. Leofwyn slaps his brother's arm and moves back to his crew. They head off, low in the mist, barely a sound made. Alfred will be behind them, keeping from making noise. Harold moves back to his own group; they fan out, Wulfric tight beside Harold. The stranger is gone, no matter, they're here. They can see the guards at the towers and ready their bows as Harold, Wulfric and twelve of the crew slip through the darkness carrying their rope ladders. They come upon the ditch, full of waste and shit and head down slowly, up to their knees in it. four men to a ladder, three towers to take, and then the rest to follow. At the sound of a clunk of the ladder's hook against the flat beam of the covered tower, the guards stir, and just as quickly fall, two arrows apiece in them.

Harold goes up the rope ladder into the first tower and finishes them. Behind him Wulfric and Hereward. They head quietly towards the next tower where Olaf, unusually nimble is finishing his man. They wait for Edwin and Harald the Dane to come through and quickly take down two men headed towards the third group. Then the fourteen of them survey the ground. Most are asleep at this hour. Just the guards on the walls and the odd man taking a piss. The barracks sit just opposite the king's great hall, and dwellings fill the compound. He looks towards the gate – no sign of Leofwyn yet. They move further across the wall, Harold himself bringing down a guard at the corner tower. Behind him the archers scale the wall. He motions for Harald the Dane and the brother Bjorn and Asbjorn to move on the gatehouse.

Just then, a cry. The guards at the gatehouse stir. Harold quietly orders his men to loose arrows on the guards. Only one goes down. Olaf, Harold and Herward move on the gatehouse guards and hack at them as half the men rush to the gate. The rest move quickly on the barracks door. Finally, Leofwyn appears at the other side of the gate shaking his head.

"Sloppy," he mouths. Harold nods. The fort is stirring and he waits for the men to get the gate open. Leofwyn moves to the barracks as Harold brings his men together. Dane axes are brought up and they charge towards the hall. Too late for stealth now. The alarm sounds as men in breeches rush out to be cut down at the barracks doors. Yelling and screams as the court wakes. They head towards the great door of the hall, Wulfric held back by Harold who races to draw the doors back before they are bolted. The guard at the door falls in a spray of blood. And Harold heaves the great oak beams back. In he charges swinging his axe. Clear the deck Harold, with your axe there. Men swept, women, no matter. Blood. Clear the hall. Take the king in chains. Or take his head. Olaf close behind and the other men pressing. Forward into the hall, servants and courtiers both panicked in the face on the onslaught. All fall before them as they move to the back of the hall. A dagger shoots out and Harld swings his axe; Olaf has the arm of the man off and he screams. They carry on through the hall to the king's chambers. Behind them shrieking and cursing, carls laughing and bellowing as they swing their great axes. Screams and the thud of axes into flesh. They crash through the door to see a fine man in his breeches climbing through a window at the top of a ladder. Gruffyd. Hereward storms through, knocking aside a woman who screams, and heads up the ladder behind the man. Others follow him as Harold sees his prey flee across the rampart.

"After him, go after him," he bellows. He drags the woman up — she is familiar. Ealdgyth of Mercia.

"Olaf!" He roars, "guard her. No one touches her. He pulls his helmet up to let her see his face.

"Harold Godwinson." He nods and heads up the ladder after his men.

"Stay right where you are lady," Olaf says. "You'll need to do what I say because there are a hundred and fifty men waiting out there and I'm the only thing between you and them."

She sits down on the king's bed and weeps. Olaf stands beside her, his axe ready for any man gone berserk. He looks towards the door as the screams pour through.

*   *   *

Gruffyd, slayer of Saxons, high king of the Welsh, dark haired and mighty, flees, hauling himself over the edge of a tower and making for the mists. Five of Harold's men give chase but he is gone, just a sprained ankle to show for their efforts.

Harold comes back down the ladder and passes Ealdgyth, called Swan-neck, and her protector. He walks into the hall, a vast timbered place now covered in bodies and gore. Men, women lie dead or twitching; the odd child remains weeping on its mother's breast. Some prisoners were taken in the melee but not many. The housecarls nod to their lord. Outside the sound of screams and iron clash on iron. He strides out. Alfred and his crews are inside the fort, he can hear the deep voice of his chief urging his men on. He greets Leofwyn, who by now has barricaded the barracks.

"Light it up," says Harold, and his brother motions to a carl to light the thatch. A wild, half naked man lurches at Harold and he turns and swings, the shaft of his axe meeting the man in the throat. He goes down and the next movement half severs his head. "Burn everything but the great hall!" Alfred has divided his men into groups of ten and they move onwards, shields up, taking down any man that moves. Resistance is slight now. Women beseeching the armed me to spare them in a language they do not understand. It is planting season, shearing too, so few folk are here. A mercy for them.

He walks back into the hall to collect the Queen. She is still sitting on her bed, drained of tears and weak.

"My husband," she asks plaintively.

"He escaped."

"Am I to be held hostage?"

"We'll take you to Liverpool where you can travel under guard to Tamworth. Your father has enough to answer for. You have no value to me as a bargaining tool, Ealdgyth." He places a bearskin over her shoulders.

"Then why…"

"Come. Bring your maid in the corner there." He drags a cowering girl up from the corner of the room and orders her to find her mistress' shoes.

Leading her by the arm through the hall, he catches her as she sees her court gutted. He spots one of his men spread out on the floor, blood drained from his face.

"Hereward! Get Sigurd out of here and go look for any other dead." Out to the sounds of panic of men hauling themselves against the barred doors of the barracks.

"Go in and get the treasure – take him," he points to a well-dressed servant kneeling in terror. "Get it all out and get some horses, then light the place up!" No need to ask them twice. He orders housecarls to drag the survivors out of the great hall. No need to burn them too. The warriors drag out survivors and pen them inside a wall of men.

Leofwyn is waiting outside, face smeared in blood.

"Sorry about the noise before, Harold." Harold shakes his head, no matter.

"Shame about the king," says Alfred. Leofwyn purses his lips.

"We're burning his capital to the ground; he's lost his court and his reputation. We'll send an army in and finish the bastard."

"Now you're talking," says Alfred.

"The ram fled like a ewe, into the mists he ran," intones Olaf. Harold grins.

"A song for the ages, then?"

"What a tale, lord."

Yes, what a tale this will make.

* * *

They gather their dead, eight so far. Two from Harold's ship, Sigurd, felled by some unknown hand in the great hall and Aethelstan, killed in the fight outside. The others they gather and haul their bodies onto horses along with the treasure they have been bagging up. Leofwyn orders carts of fodder to be placed along the walls of the fort and they light them up. Shields are gathered from the armoury across from the barracks, and where they can the breachers find mail and sundry armour to protect them. Helping Ealdgyth onto a Horse, Harold orders the men into formation.

"We lit up a bee's nest down by the harbour, Lord," Alfred notes. There are men down there – they must hurry. They have enough horses for two crews but dividing the group now could be costly so they march out as a unit as quickly as possible. There are noises out in the fields, probably men coming in from the harvest. Too late to save the fort, but even stragglers pose a danger. They head to the shore and the town, the shouts of men and women disordered now. The journey takes a tense hour at a fast march. Men are streaming in small groups up towards the burning fort and Harold leads the mounted men against them. They fall easily even in the dark screaming under trampling horse. A stray arrow takes out another man; they are quick to gather him and place him on a horse. The rest of the men keep tight formation down the path. No need for stealth now. Halfway to the ships they meet their first pocket of organized resistance. Some thirty men organized into a wall, barely visible under the half-moon. The footmen form up in a shield wall and inch forward as other fire arrows into the night. Harold takes a group of horsemen left and Leofwyn to the right. The younger brother charges his horse to outflank them ahead of his men and piles into the Welsh soldiers just as the footmen make contact. Almost too early and almost dismounted by the shock. He swings his axe hard into the neck of the nearest man as the two walls shudder. Harold comes next and quick work is made of the resistance. He grins as Leofwyn raises an apologetic hand. The wounded are quickly dispatched much to Ealdgyth's horror as Olaf grips her arm to stop her falling.

"Lord," says the big man, "I am done watching the lady – can someone else, do it? I'm missing the fight."

Harold nods and Ceolwulf jumps up behind her onto the horse and muscles her forward so he can keep her balance.

They check for enemies behind them and reform, marching onto the village. Here the horsemen scatter all in their path and the men on foot light up the houses. Leofwyn and seven other race down to the beach where a fierce fight is happening between the guards and some settlers. They plough into the Welsh and hack at the men in various states of dress. Sailors have gathered from the ships and are throwing stones and axes over. Some five men are lost here, but the ships are safe. He motions to the sailors to return to the ships and gathers torches before heading to the Welsh harbour. Harold joins him here and they dispatch the last pockets of resistance. Quickly, methodically they light up Welsh ships, forming a wall behind the men working with archers posted behind the shields. The stench of smoke is suffocating, and men are hacking at the hulls of beached boats. Townsfolk are gathering now, unarmed and beseeching mercy. The cordon of men stays tight around and the horsemen dismount. It is time to leave. They perform a quick headcount and ask for the dead. Dragging their bodies, they move back to the ships. The Welsh have given up resisting and armed men drop their weapons and raise hands. Inching towards the ships they throw their axes and shields onboard, haul the dead and treasure off the horse and secure them on ship and push as hard as they can to move the ships off. They take to oar in the shallows, being careful not to lose a man to the waves. Taking to oar the men use the last of their strength to haul away from the shore. Harold and his crew are last, formed up and backing out onto their ships, archers posted and firing the odd warning shot. Then they too are gone. Black specks on deep grey moving away from the fierce glow of fires.

* * *

They put in at Liverpool's fine little harbour. Across the river, Northumbria and Tostig's mess.

"Our seafaring is over for now lads; it's quicker to ride back with these winds." Harold says to his men. He instructs the sailors to pick up a few good men as crew from Blackpool and make their way back to Bristol and Bosham. The housecarls gather their gear. He picks ten men to take the dead to

"Arm up, men." They form up in pairs and don their mail and bracers, each man fixing his partners gear at the back, binding their windings around their legs and fetching their shields. The cream of the might of Wessex form up before their Lord. Four abreast they turn and march through the harbour of Liverpool, here in Mercia, as if in Wales. Folk are shunted aside. Baskets of fish and bread scattered without thought. Here Wessex marches with a humbled queen in tow. On to the gridded streets they move. Folk stare and mutter but no one dares shove or throw so much as a stick at the crew. A hundred and fifty strong, not a single man lost, save one limping; such is the lure of the shearing that even a king cannot call an army to encircle him.

Here comes the Reeve on horseback with a guard he's rustled up. Harold and his brother move to the fore. Word will have gone out and a levy summoned.

"What men are you?"

"We come with your lord's daughter."

"And 'we' are?"

"Earl Harold, of Wessex."

"Earl…" The reeve is stunned. A slender man on a fine warhorse, more suited to a palfrey.

"We found the lady Ealdgyth in a Welsh fortress and decided to bring her back to her own folk, as sis fitting."

"Lady…"

"Well say a whole sentence, man. Bring her up, gently now men, gently."

The thin man hauls himself ungainly from his steed. "Lady Ealdgyth, my lady, are you well? Did they?"

Before she could demure, Harold's hand is upon his shoulder like a harness.

"No, cur, they did not."

"My lord…Lord, Harold. I meant."

"Yet so you did. We bring the daughter of Mercia back safe to her folk and here some reeve dares to call us rapists."

"Lord, let's hang him by his feet and move on."

"No need, no need." Harold grins at the terrified reeve. What good would the man be in a fight?

"We need horses, reeve."

"I can have horses for you and the lady brought, lord."

"Two hundred, reeve." The reeve stares at this foreign earl and his invading force with a mixture of disbelief and fearful outrage.

"No lord."

"Two hundred horses, like the one you almost fell off."

"Fell? Earl Harold, you are not lord here. Losing two hundred war horses could endanger us, lord."

"But I am escorting your lady back to Tamworth."

"My home is in Wales," she pipes up, ashen faced still.

"Where is your husband, Ealdgyth," Leofwyn asked.

"Wherever you chased him to."

"Such are the mercies of the Godwins, lady, that we take a detour to ensure your safety."

"You make no sense, you are the cause of all of this."

"No Ealdgyth," says Harold, "we are the cure. Your husband broke the peace and made war on Wessex to unite his own kind. The end will come for him and I do not want your blood on my family's hands. The kingdom must be united under Edward. That is my pledge to the king."

"The outcome, Ealdgyth, could have been far worse," says Leofwyn. "You are better off among your own than with your husband. Even he would agree, wherever he's hiding." She stares at their handsome honest faces, innocent of bloodshed and horror, in disbelief.

"Lord Harold," says the Reeve, "Why is Lady Ealdgyth with you?"

"We burned Rhuddlan to the ground."

"You burned…"

"Yes, they attacked my home and burned it and killed most of the people inside." Harold raises his hand.

"Lord Harold."

"Earl."

"Ealdorman Harold, this puts Mercia at risk, surely? To burn the capital with—with just this group? Is this true? Taking good warhorse further weakens us." Around them the people have gathered to hear them.

"Just this band of men Lord?" A middle-aged woman looks in disbelief at the group before her.

"Just this band. Good men lost."

"Danish Harold sprained his ankle too," Olaf piped up to chuckles from the crowd. There were scattered cheers made all the more flattering by the Reeve's angry look. Mercia's alliance is the word here.

"Where is the Welsh King then?"

"He ran naked into the night like a sheep." Again, cheers and laughter.

"Shame our lot didn't do anything."

"Too busy bitching about Northumbria," someone shouted from the crowd.

"Olaf, Winston, get some horses and go to Blackpool stables with a few men. The rest of you, let's get the dead buried there before they stink. I need their names noted – Hereward you write them down and get their families' names. Alfred, accompany the Reeve here and find us the balance." The Reeve is caught in the bearlike embrace of Alfred's arm and escorted to his mare. Harold goes back to the boats and looks over the dead laid out under skins and blankets on the pier. He touches each of them on the breast. The best men in England. His men gather around and kneel in prayer. Their brothers are gone now, died gloriously in battle and they can move on in pride. Personal effects will be taken and placed in pouches for their families and a geld will be paid.

So, they requisition horses for their crew. One hundred and fifty from Mercia and fifty from Tostig. They order graves to be dug in Liverpool churchyard and have the local priests perform their rites. Some of the men openly weep, faces still covered in blood and soot. No shame in weeping here. They stay the night in Liverpool, taking over two small inns and the main town hall. Ealdgyth is placed with her maid, an English girl of fine appearance and delicate features, under guard. Local women are brought to serve her in a hastily made-up quarter.

"There's going to be trouble," Alfred, who spent the day requisitioning horses from a ten-mile sweep, stroked his greying moustaches.

"They'll send whatever housecarls and fyrd out, but we can travel with them as escort and head down to Winchester. Let's keep the whoring to a minimum." Alfred shook his head thoughtfully.

"If we had landed in Blackpool and headed through Northumbria…"

"We might be lying with our throats slit or a Scottish raiding party on our tails." Tostig's mess.

"It's not my place to question lord."

"Question away my friend, my answer will be the same – not a man lost and his capital burned to the ground. Perhaps the Welsh will see to Gruffyd and save us the trouble. Yes, it was shame we didn't catch him."

"I suppose we can't complain, lord."

"Now I'm sore about it."

"Sorry Harold."

That night they feast in Liverpool. Weapons are kept from the hall and housecarl. Lord and sailor drank as brothers. The next day, bleary eyed and happy, the hall stinks of ale and piss and the housecarls stretching their limbs with the whores of the town and some free folk too lying about them. Rousing his men, they get up with the ease of men who lived the hard life and the soft life – the needs of the warrior. Moving outside they are confronted by a thegn and a band of mounted men.

"Where is the lady Ealdgyth?"

*   *   *

On the road to Tamworth, through the green fields, this great band of nobles and housecarls ride. Men from Mercia and Wessex rubbing shoulders; the Mercians wide eyed with disbelief at the raid. The Thegn, Aethelstan, named after the great uniter, grins at Harold.

"I want with my whole heart to believe you, Earl Harold, but Christ how did one hundred and fifty men burn Rhuddlan to the ground?"

"It's actually not that large," Leofwyn answers. Aethelstan's wife is from Wessex, a thegn's daughter, loyal to Harold and Godwin before him. Family.

"It's large enough," Harold laughs at his brother's mock humility. Ealdgyth, called Swan Neck for her elegant and lithe form, bows her head.

"And Lady Ealdgyth is back with her family now," the thegn nods approvingly. "I never understood that marriage, all respect due to my lord Aelfgar."

"That's a matter for the king later; regardless she is safe and well as can be expected despite the unpleasantness she witnessed."

"One thing can be said of Earl Harold," she almost spits the words, "he is not lying. He burned the buildings in Rhuddlan to the ground, and when he was done, he set haycarts against the walls and burned them too."

"And the whole place lit up like a bonfire."

"Majestic," Aethelred murmurs. "Apologies Lady, I know it must have been hard for you. Majestic. You know, vikings attack villages, monasteries, the defenceless. You, Earl, sorry Earls, you attacked a whole fucking fortress."

"And then, my lord," Alfred interjects, "we went down to the harbour and burned their boats too."

"It was really something," Leofwyn says.

"Yes, it was," his brother agrees.

The group pause at Warrington and Knutsford, causing dismay to the local thegns, who have two hundred men foisted on their good will. Harold offers a surety of a royal disbursement, "to be paid upon request."

"You know Harold," says Leofwyn scratching at his stubble. "We should organize some kind of stables relay across the country. We can send men up and down to bolster defences with some kind of distributed stables or inns."

"I like that. Good luck getting the Mercians to agree to it – no offense, Aethelstan. I need a bath too. You stink."

The next morning, fresh as could be achieved without new clothes, the men and their charges depart. They ride along the paths, ages old, morning dew lapping the feet of their horses; across the Mersey and through the fields and marshes of Cheshire. An untamed land, sparsely populated and ancient seeming, as if the ghosts of the first men teemed around the marshes, waiting to drag them down to some ungodly underworld. Still, beautiful, and a reminder of all they have achieved in Wessex, these Englishmen. Onwards, to the dense and ancient Delamere Forest, sticking to roman roads, and paths cleared by locals. Carls to the front and sides, watchful of ambushes. They ride for an hour through the clearings, every sound of boar and bird a warning, and a call to the hunt. Light abbreviates through the foliage, and they mind their horses' nerves.

Out then into the mild light of the Staffordshire afternoon. The land rising before them as they cross the hills and lightly cultivated fields. Scattered hamlets cross their path; one farmer staring up at these familiar men, looks up and asks.

"Is there a war on, then?"

"A war? Not for you my friend, no need to fear," Harold grins at the man. "We're just passing through." But there will be war now.

On to Eccleshall. Aethelstan recommended it as a suitable waypoint, secure and ample pasture for the horses. Bishop Leofwyn is not present, being away at Lichfield; a perfect choice for these men of Wessex and far less tedious than dealing with the bishop.

"We can't have two Leofwyns anyway," quips Olaf.

"We have five Harolds, and four Svens," says Leofwyn.

There the prior greets them with surprise and fear. Aethelstan dismounts, the hard men around him motionless, save for the odd twitch of a horse.

"We have here Ealdgyth of Mercia, Queen of Wales, and her escort, myself, Earl Harold of Wessex, his brother, Earl Leofwyn."

"This is most unexpected. I must send word to the bishop."

"We'll be off in the morning, prior. We have need of fodder and beds for the men, and private quarters for the lady and her servant."

"And the earls, lord."

"We can sleep with the men, they've seen it all." Harold dismounted and clapped his hand on the prior's shoulder like a bear's paw on a child. The prior shuddered.

That night they helped themselves to the prior's stores of meat and ale; the men clean their armour and call for fresh windings for their legs. Harold and his brother go to table with the prior, Aethelstan, and Ealdgyth, still quiet within herself.

"Let us pray," says the prior.

"Benedic, Domine, nos et haec tua dona,
quae de tua largitate sumus sumpturi,
per Christum Dominum nostrum. Amen.

Harold and Lefowyn dutifully nod and mouth amen, before they tuck into their meal of rabbit and veal. Aethelstan remains half-bowed in prayer for a few moments more. Harold and Leofwyn grin at each other like boys; as he looks up, Aethelstan blushes at the gentle mockery of these great men. Having repeated the tale, the prior sits silent, his eyes flitting between the earls.

"This could call a horror upon Mercia, lords."

"You mean England, prior?" Harold eyed the man with an amused gaze.

"Our lord is father-in-law to the Welsh king – his daughter…"

"Is safe, and untouched."

"And without the burden of a Welsh pup," Leofwyn notes. Ealdgyth scowls at the slight.

"I always saw you as a man of honour, Harold. A good and honest man. Not a merciless killer." The swiftness of war, the blur of an axe, movement of men before and to the side; no time to think.

Clear the decks. Mind the man to your left; watch your step always; one eye on the deck.

"Harold is the best man in England, Ealdgyth. Whatever his people need, he provides. When there is danger, he is first to action; now the king is…older, Harold has become his axe and shield. Whatever the king orders, he delivers…"

"Unlike his father," she interrupts Leofwyn.

"Perhaps, but true nonetheless." Harold's expression is calm and unflustered. "Gruffyd attacked Wessex, repeatedly. And Harold took action, at great risk to himself, to spare the people of your – adopted country from the wrath of England. The wrath that would devastate the land."

"My father, Mercia, have a treaty with Wales."

"Mercia is not a country anymore, Ealdgyth," chided Harold. "The king has treaties, and we must honour them. Your father struck his own deal at the expense of his country. And now we have acted."

"And my husband is still alive."

"And king of the ashes only. If we had captured him, we would have saved his people the job of ending him." She shudders at this blank statement.

"You speak like you are lord of Mercia too. I must excuse myself." The men nod slightly as she pushes her chair out and leaves.

"Well," says the prior after a long silence, "how was the rabbit?"

*　　*　　*

They take the main road down to Tamworth, the prior having already sent word to his bishop of the Earls' exploits. By now news would be trickling through Mercia, on its way to Northumbria and down to Wessex.

"Gyrth will be jealous," Leofwyn noted as the rode leisurely with their charge.

"He'll have his fun now," Harold says. His brother gives him a long enquiring look, but he rides on impassively. Ealdgyth, riding silently next to them speaks up.

"The prior told me my mother will be in Coventry. I would prefer to go there."

"Now she tells us," Olaf with a loud theatrical sigh. A hundred men laugh and she reddens.

"Coventry it is then," Harold says, the men groan. They are eager to be back at Winchester. At the large, fortified town of Tamworth, they stop for a short time to buy tunics, breeches and windings for the men. The stables here are called upon to swap out tire or unfit horses, with the promissory notes carefully prepared in the King's name. They are traveling light, the treasure from their haul hidden in the ships' hold under gear and blankets, but the earl has his purse, and notes for the king. They set off in the early afternoon, Aethelstan making good with the local thegns and Reeves in the small time he has. Harold remains outside the city walls for now, his men dismounted and bored in the light rain. Their armour is on the spare horses and the men of Wessex share stories with their Mercian counterparts. There is no tension between these men – they are paid men and proud of their service but there is no rivalry off the field, and no formal war between them. Most are of the raid – few would dare what Harold did, with so small a group.

"The way back to the boats was hardest," Alfred intoned to the groups that listened. Fighting men running confused, people too. We burned their houses at random, and marched as a group, men with shields up in front."

"A wonder more weren't killed."

"It was the time for planting and shearing, so men were scattered. Also, I think they just couldn't get it through their heads they were being attacked. Mercia being so close."

"They forgot about Wessex," laughs Leofwyn; and the men laugh heartily with the earl.

"You mean England," says Aethelstan smiling.

They finally drop Ealdgyth with her mother, a stout woman with scant resemblance to her elegant and lovely daughter. The lords stop in silence ruminating on it, while Ealdgyth looks back at them with an aggrieved expression. After some discussion with her daughter, Aelgifu walks up to the dismounted lords.

"Thegn Aethelstan, greetings." She looks at Harold and Leofwyn, "Earls Harold and Leofwyn, I suppose I should thank you for not defiling my daughter when you burned her home to the ground."

"We accept your thanks, lady, and wish you and your husband peace and prosperity," Harold says mildly. She bristles. "Say now, can we trouble you for fresh water and perhaps some ale or wine?"

"No ale or wine for your men, lords, I know their reputation. Water, yes. I'll have the thralls come out and refill your men's skins."

They nod pleasantly. The men groan at the absence of ale.

"My husband will know of this."

"Your husband is at court and of course will hear it from our own lips. That his daughter is safe, but…business may be a bit tight for a while."

As the skins are filled, Aethelstan makes pleasant conversation with the stout lady and agrees to stay for supper with his men. Here they will part ways, these brothers on the road, back to their domains and the awkward joinings a stitched-together nation brings. This is the end then: Harold gives a final look at Ealdgyth, fair and graceful, yet ever against him now, and mounts his horse after a friendly hug with Aethelstan. The men wave their goodbyes; perhaps next time they will fight as brothers. The legend is told now and will pass through the land—Harold's raid on Rhuddlan.

Bosham & The North

It is Terce. Tostig and the king kneel together in the king's private chapel. The floor is hard under their knees and the simple furnishings contrast the richness of the palace. They pray as one, the priest at the altar of the King's private chapel leading those who know the prayers as well as him. When they are finished, they remain in silence. Finally, the king speaks up:

"Tosty, the situation in the North is tenuous. Malcolm is another Griffin; building alliances with him is inviting the wolf to the sheep pen."

"Lord, I have done all that you asked, turning the remnants of Danelaw into an English shire, bringing order and profit. But the people chafe against our yoke. I have scarcely enough good men to restrain them and the thegns are murderous in some parts, especially on the border. This yoke is hard for them to bear, and they see me as the sole instigator."

"You have done well, but perhaps a gentler hand is needed. And Malcom, your…friend, must be stopped, Tosty. He must."

"Malcom's raids cause the border thegns to focus on the Scots. I know, it is a callous thing for an earl to say, but he is a welcome distraction from these men who would slit my throat as soon as offer their hides."

"My son, we have known each other these long years and you are pious and noble, but we cannot have disquiet in the North. I thought your half-Danish heritage would prove a positive."

"Lord, they see me as a southerner, Danish mother or not. We had success at first but, lord, forgive me, your demands are high and my means to collect are limited. York and the regions around are mine, though, Lord. I can call on them in a heartbeat."

"I will think on it, Tosty, my son. But do try to visit Northumbrian soon. It is important to have a strong fist in a velvet glove. Now where is Harold? He has been gone weeks now."

"He was planning some raid, Lord; I hear Alfred and his men rode out to meet him. I don't know what else—he can be tight-lipped about these things."

"Your brother is a strong man and a good man; perhaps the best of us, my son. But he has a hot head."

"He has to keep moving Lord, it is his way, planning, moving, acting always and planning while acting. It's as if his mind would run away from him if he didn't keep going."

"That, exactly," says the king. "I do hope he hasn't run into trouble with so few men."

"I have seen my brother take down four men at a time, lord, he is like a bear; as we are said to be descended from one."

"A bear who does not hibernate or sit still."

They rise and make their way to the hall for the King to greet his courtiers in the morning. The king gives a fond half-smile to Tostig.

"All will be fine, Tosty. Trust in the Lord and visit your people."

Tostig nodded. As the king moved on, he pursed his lips, and his shoulders stooped slightly. Trapped in Edward's

As they descend from the private chapel, they hear a commotion.

"Earl Harold! Harold is here!"

The members of the court here at this hour rise up to hear of the Earl's appearance. The king, still active at sixty, hurries down. Servants and members of the court both, bow their heads to the king. Tostig follows swiftly behind.

"Harold, what news?"

"Lord king. We raided Rhuddlan and burned the place to the ground."

There are cheers from the crowd.

"How many men, Harold, surely not one ship?"

"Five, lord."

How many men, two hundred?"

"One hundred and fifty, lord," says Leofwyn.

"One hundred and fifty? And where are these men? To the ground?"

"Yes, and their ships as we returned. They are outside, Lord."

"Then I shall visit them. Marvellous, Harold, marvellous! And the king, this Griffin?"

"Gruffyd, Lord," says Harold, "It means the same thing. He escaped, Lord, leaving his wife behind."

Aelfgar, followed closely by his sons, bursts into the great hall.

"Harold! Harold! What did you do to my daughter?" He grabs onto Harold's shoulder, who swings round and knocks him down like a child. The hall is silent. Edwin and Morcar reach for their knives, but Leofwyn is quick and puts a knife to their father's throat.

"Calm, lads, calm, not in the King's presence," says Harold, reaching down to pick the earl up as if a wool sack.

"Aelfgar, calm yourself and do not lay hands on another earl again. Especially not this one. He could tear you limb from limb," chastises the king.

The sons sheath their knives as Leofwyn stares them down. Tostig now moves to his side.

"Your daughter—is well and with her mother."

"And undefiled?"

"No." The court is stunned into silence. After a pause, "You sold her to a Welsh King, so her purity is suspect." Men in the court bellow with laughter and the king gives a cunning smile.

"I see what you did there, Harold," he says.

"Lord." Harold says smiling.

The court is gathered around now, the humiliated Aelfgar up on his feet and accepting a firm handshake from his rival. The greens, blues and reds of the courtiers' tunics mingle into a wash of colour as they gather round the earl. Tostig puts his arm around Leofwyn, who grins at him.

"Say, Earl Harold," says one courtier, "What on earth gave you the idea of raiding Rhuddlan?"

"This man here," he says, pointing to Aelfgar. "Gruffyd thinks he can get away with raiding Wessex and Cornwall while trading with Aelfgar. He expected a strike along the Irish sea, so I figured a strike on the capital, being so close to Mercia, would be unexpected."

"And you were right," says the king. Harold nods. There is applause." Harold, the hunt I organized…"

"No matter, Lord, I took time to visit on the way. It was necessary and a useful distraction."

"A feast," the king declares loudly, raising his arms. "Tomorrow, we feast. Today, we go to the map room, Harold, if you are not tired."

"No Lord, not overly. But where is Gyrth?"

"Doing his job in East Anglia," says the king pointedly. Tostig smarts but nods.

There is much backslapping and praise as Harold and his brothers follow the king through the hall to the map room.

*   *   *

"So, Harold, what is the plan now?"

"We will Harry them, Lord. Land and sea."

"No babes or slaves from the children of God," says Wulfstan.

Harold scowls.

But the king looks up at Harold and gives a look - that same look almost 15 years ago.

He nods. "Just the men and buildings then."

"And Tostig…" says the king.

"I am with you in all things, Lord," says Tostig.

"Tosty," says Harold with a smirk – the king's nickname.

Tostig rolled his eyes slightly. "What are my—orders?"

"No. You will lead on land with Gyrth. Leofwyn and I will take to sea." The younger brothers beam.

"Excellent idea Harold and very generous. Independent armies – look Tostig, your own command at last," The king is beaming also.

"From Mercia?"

"I cannot have it, we have trade," Aelfgar says, "And marriage—my daughter."

"Again, with his daughter," Leofwyn groans. "She is safe and sound." Edward nods approvingly at the man who used to bounce on his knee, receive the mildest of the king's thin-sticked thrashings to appease his father's angry hand. Still young but he has grown even in this short time.

'Collect Northumbrians and Mercians, under the Fyrd law and strike in my name,' says Edward. 'Enough Aelfgar. We are as one now. One kingdom.'

The earl of Mercia scowled. "It's late to be decisive, king."

The room descends into a shocked silence.

"I will pretend you didn't say that," Edward says mildly, yet his eyes are ice. That ice that exiles.

"Well," says Harold breaking the silence, "we'll take enough sheep to have a roaring wool trade for the next few years. And don't worry Aelfgar, you'll get your cut for the loss of business for the short time we deal with Gruffyd. Now, to the real business. Lord, you will need to call up the Fyrd. Tostig – you will be in charge of the supply chain over land. I think Tamworth is your starting point. Gather the men there. Use Liverpool as a supply route. Leofwyn and I will organize the ship Fyrd – Leofwyn, I want you to get down to Southampton and organize the navy; but first have messengers sent to all the major ports. We will need sixty to one hundred longboats – standard fashion: sailors at the oars and warriors to remain fresh on board." Even the King nods. "From Tamworth, cut west and form a wide path with the men. Burn and pillage, but not everything and keep communication tight—the Welsh are excellent at ambush, and we can't afford to lose men in small groups – it will be bad for their spirit if pockets of men disappear. Our main supply centres are York, Tamworth, Southampton and Bristol. I want the supply lines kept in check but, Tostig, you should live off the land too. Where is Gyrth anyway?"

"He's managing affairs and seeing the Walsingham Shrine."

"Shrine?"

"A venerable noblewoman called Richeldis had a vision of the nativity and built a shrine," says Edward in wonder.

"So Gyrth is coming closer to God," Tostig smiles.

"About time too," says Leofwyn grinning at Harold.

"We need Gyrth with Tostig, and we need him to provision the East Anglia fyrd. Alfred – have men go to him and give our instructions after this. I will write them down myself."

"In runes," Laughed Leofwyn. Harold laughed along.

"Tosty, I will make land at Aberdovy…Aberdeffy… here," he points on the map. "This place. I will leave half the navy to harry any remaining Welsh ships and trade. You will march inland, and we will assemble there with two supply chains at our backs and an exit route if needed."

"Where you will assume command," says Tostig.

"Exactly. We will march up the Dyfi valley and meet at Machynlleth and lay waste or seek their surrender. If we still haven't made our point, we will live off the land and stick to the lowlands until their backs are broke."

Stigand, quiet as the warriors planned, muses "Why not just bring the Welsh to heel, Lord, and make them a region of England?"

"To conquer Welsh soil is not to conquer the Welsh. If England was conquered, would it lie down?"

"I think we know the answer to that is, yes, Lord," says Tostig, "Look to Cnut. A few battles, certainly, but for the most part we English prospered and change dour allegiance to Cnut, more-so perhaps than to his predecessors."

"'We English' married Danes and made…us," says Leofwyn.

"These Welsh are different. They have been here for longer than us and have their mountains and heartland. You cannot purge them…"

"They are Christian!" Wulfnof interjects.

"Yes, that too, but you can take their lowlands and for what? To spend your wealth and resources defending against cattle raids and slaughter of entire settling families. No, we would be cooped up like chickens in our walled coops, going out in large groups to fight ghosts, and watching our fields burn every harvest." Harold shook his head.

"Did you not apprehend some nihlings in the woods of Exeter," Wulfnoth persisted.

"Men of little worth or knowledge of fighting. These Welsh Have history before us, before the Romans. You cannot conquer such a people; you can only trap yourself in a cage while they rape your daughters and hang your sons' balls across their noses. No, we harry. We become the Welsh and the Viking. We have burned their capital, and we will burn their ports and their farmsteads and let their armies scurry around trying to put out the fires. And then we will combine and meet them on the field of battle and force their king to kneel; or better, we take his head."

Aelfgar smarted.

"Damn, Harold, you have a strong hatred of this man."

"Hatred, no, deep respect, yes. He united this warring rabble into a nation and not a race. Just like Alfred did. I've talked with him, remember? Shared his cup, made peace with him. He must be stopped before he makes us build another dike around the border. Or worse, makes a pact with Tostig's Malcom and sets the borders on fire. He's also a damned nuisance to our trade and people."

"Malcolm would not side with Gruffyd, this I know." Tostig stands awkwardly.

"Malcom raids Northumberland and you go hunting with hm the next day," Edwin, heir to Mercia stares at Tostig.

"Not Malcolm, border thegns."

"Under Malcolm's rule. There is no difference, Tostig. They break the peace, and you say your prayers and let it alone." Tostig gives Edwin a sour look.

"We can deal with Malcolm next," says Harold. "We will fight in late spring. Time to assemble to Fyrd, if you will, Lord." Tostig breathes a long breath.

Edward nods heartily. "Let's teach him too, Harold. We can get a tribute from him after you've bested him again."

"A weregild would be good lord, but we need a stable and humbled Scotland to our North. The Scots can rein their raiders in. The Welsh will turn on themselves without Gruffyd holding them together by force of will."

The king claps his hands. "Excellent, Harold. Your strategy is complete. Pity we didn't capture Gruffyd in the raid, but he is weakened, and you and Tosty will force the Welsh to decide between their farms and their king. Come father," he says beckoning to a priest who had been scribing. "I want the fyrd called out for all of England. Write it up for each region and we will send the Sheriffs out."

"Now Aelfgar," Harold places his arms warmly around the shorter man's shoulder. "You know our plan, you are a part of our plans, your son will join the campaign, and we shall take the men of your land. Your daughter is safe, and she has no children by her husband." Tostig, Leofwyn move in around him and he shudders. "Are you with us?"

There is silence.

"Well," says the king, "answer the man."

"I…am with you."

"So forcefully put, Aelfgar, I almost believe you. He is kin, of a kind, this Gruffyd, but we are your folk. When the king calls up the fyrd, as my father...as we," gesturing to his brothers, "learned to our doom, they come whether or not their earl wishes it."

The king beams at Harold. "So wise, my boy."

"Thank you, lord. Now, about the succession..."

They all laugh heartily and the King motions for dismissal.

*   *   *

Harold and Tostig walk together. Harold links his brother's arm.

"Tostig, you are close to Edward, like the son he never had."

"A disappointment of a son."

"So what? If the man prays with you, hunts with you, walks with you, smiles at your successes and mourns your failures, I think you have it good, brother. He loves you far more than me."

"But he respects you."

"Yes, and he has my loyalty, since he came back. I am not father; I know my place as the second son."

Tostig nods and puts his hand over his brother's.

"But Tostig, the thing about Edward...you ask for permission. I act and then I tell. You need to own and not seek his advice. When he tells you--wait—do this, act like that, he will change his mind and ask why you did not do this new thing. If you follow Edward's orders to the letter year after year and you have chaos."

"The North…"

"You did as you were told. You might still make it right. Find a means of getting gold. Go North and raid Malcolm back and see how the bastard likes it. Lower taxes on the troublesome. Find peace at York. They love you there." Tostig cocks a brow, "I have men who make it their business to know, brother. I am not that cunning—I need the thieves and spies around me to seem so."

"But when you're wrong…"

"I take my licks like I took them from father. I bow my head. I act again and I try to mend it. But look brother – I got Wessex, Gyrth got East Anglia, Wyn got, well whatever he got. You got a land still mired in the Danelaw, resistant to taxes, resistant to rule from the south. You, half-Danish, the perfect fit. And you listened to Edward, and you took the whole thing on at once. And you won."

"For a while."

Harold stops walking.

"Yes, that exactly. You win by holding men by their shoulders, by gradually easing corruption, listening to the problems. Hanging a few nihlings. Purging the worst lot of robbers and thieves. Promoting the capable and appeasing the established thegns. It's hard, brother. But we could win against the Welsh and build our nation there, and they would never stop. They would never rest. These northerners are just the same. What you did in those first years was something to behold. Better even than I might have done. I had an easy entrance to Wessex. I grew up among them, like you."

"Everyone calls you Harold here. They spit "earl" at me in the North."

"It would be hard to demand "Lord" from people who caught me stealing apples and falling dead drunk in their fields. I am as much their son as your brother. My burden is to be better, yours, to build."

"So, what do I do?"

"Make your choice, but Tostig, I beg you, stay away from Malcolm. I do not want my brother to be another Aelfgar."

They hug and Tostig smiles a rare smile.

"Brother…"

"I know, me too, Tostig. You know what I do like," A French servant is passing by, looking nervously at the lords.

"What is that, Harold?" Tostig rolls his eyes.

"Knocking down a Frenchman once in a while, but there are so few. He half lunges at the servant who cowers and hurries on.

"You'll hear from Edward," Tostig shakes his head.

"I'm to Bosham. Take the family. Make the boys men."

"I'll go North, perhaps."

They hug and part. Harold looks after his brother and shakes his head sadly.

Leofwyn comes up from a tactful distance.

"You are welcome, with the wife of course. I mean it is your home too."

"I'll take your offer; my house is too far for my sore body to manage. I'll fetch the wife."

Harold grins. Almost like the old days.

* * *

Harold walks to the great door of his quarters. The guards part ways and his family are gathered in the small hall to meet him. Edith greets her husband at the door to their home near the king's court. They kiss and he holds her the way he did the first time. The boys stand back.

"Harold, that was brave, but my god, five ships to take on the capital."

"It really wasn't that big," says Harold grinning. He is unshaved but his moustache is still bold across his face and rubs her when he kisses her again. "We didn't get Gruffyd."

"Never mind, we missed you. You didn't even say goodbye."

"The king's hunt…"

"Still, Harold."

"Secrecy was everything this time, my love. Aelfgar is at court, and I had to keep it close."

"What now?"

"Bosham. Tostig, Win and Gyrth can take care of logistics. We'll start to move in a month.

"So, we have you for a month."

"About that, yes."

"When will you ever rest, Harold?"

"When I choke on my food." She shakes her head at him and holds him tight.

"Boys! Gytha. Mor." The boys come out, Godwin and Edmund tall and slim, Magnus still fighting for his height. Gytha lithe like her mother, not stout; it is good, she'll make a fine woman. His mother comes out, tall and ruddy, once very pretty and well set. A breeder of men, his father says.

"Mor," he says, warmly hugging her.

"Søn, Du er hjemme." You are home. "And Win too with Godgifu."

"Yes, Win is coming home to Bosham; he can go between home and Southampton to organize the fleet."

"No Tostig," his mother asks fretfully.

"He should go North," Tostig, the favourite son.

The boys come and greet their father. The news has travelled, and they are in awe beyond their normal respect. He claps them on their shoulders and pulls them to him one at a time. To Gytha he gives a thump on the shoulder, and she punches him as hard as she can in his chest.

It is time to rest. He takes his wife by hand and heads to his chamber.

* * *

The next day, the feast is prepared. The great hall is cleared of the royal hangings and statuary and the tables are prepared. The kitchens are expanded by tents and servants swarm the back quarters of the king's hall. The slaughterhouse has been busy, and butchers are at work on their cuts. Cured meats are brought from every shop and household that can afford it, and the bakers have been at their bread making for a day now. A single order and the world is all bustle. Everyone will join the feast across the city in makeshift tents and on the street.

Prayers are said and the host assembles in the early afternoon. The great hall is filled with men and women, so many that the hearths are put out. The king, dressed in his purple tunic, sits at the head of the table, Harold to his right and the earls assembled down both sides; their wives interspersed, and the children sat at tables to the rear. The great and minor thegns, visitors to court, all dressed in their brightest tunics, gold armlets and chains denoting their wealth. Swords and axes are outside, save for the trusted Housecarls, all denied ale and wine, ready to calm disorder or manage a fair fight.

Edward rises, his great frame imposing and his voice deep.

"These past weeks, the Welsh King Griffin was pit to flight. His capital was burned. His soldiers slain." There are cheers that are caught up by the people outside and passing through the streets until it seems the whole city roars in waves.

"Earl Harold has planned and executed this raid with his brave brother Leofwyn and his men. With the utmost secrecy they came upon Griffin's capital at night and laid waste to it. Such is the glory to England that these Welsh were caught sleeping. Truly this man is descended from bears!"

"Harold, Harold," goes the chant, men thumping the table. Harold rises, knowing to bow his head to the king and accept the glory with humility.

"By the grace of our King, Edward, we achieved a victory worthy of our people. And we sent Gruffyd running out naked as a shorn sheep into the night." The men laugh heartily. So much the better, he wishes he had Gruffyd's head. Harold nods to the crowd and sits to more thunderous banging of fists, horns and ornate cups. The ale and wine began to spill across the tables.

"Now we are to war!" Shouts Edward. "Earl Tosty will lead the land battle and Harold will take to ship and harry the Welsh coastline."

"War, War," goes the cry.

"We will show them how the English fight when we are crossed and crossed again, and Earl Aelfgar will present Mercia as the staging area for the land campaign." Aelfgar stands and nods. There are murmurs from the crowd. "And now, my Christian brothers and sisters, my English folk, my friends. We drink—to War and the end of Griffin!"

"War, War," goes the cry.

The day passes in feasting, boasting and drinking. Harold is pressed to lift a man with one arm. He does it twice, much to the delight of the women. Two thegns settle a land dispute with staves, the housecarls forming a ring as they batter each other senseless to the cheers of the crowds. A Welsh minstrel attached to Aelfgar's retinue is dragged out and made to sing in a dress. All the Welsh victory songs and more. The poor man is pelted with food and cups and is saved from a beating by a drunk thegn, who thinks the war is underway. The rooms sway in a thousand eyes and outside the city begins to stream with waste and piss. Fights break out and the odd fire starts. All is well.

A French minstrel is brought to satisfy the king, but the looks of his earls cut short the crooning, and the men begin to sing their songs of war in English and Danish. French servants scuttle about, cuffed by rough hands as they try to do their work. The king tolerates this, he lost that fight, but the people love him today as a father, as they love Harold as Harold, the keeper of the realm. The king places his arm around Harold and kisses him on the cheek. All is well.

All the while Tostig sits, drinking temperately, smiling softly at his brother, raising his cup along with the rest, Judith, his wife, by his side, clutching his knee and maintaining her gaze on him the whole while. Leofwyn pats his brother on the shoulder and grins. Thumping Harold and kissing his wife the while. Men pass by the Earls, slapping Harold drunkenly on the back and leaning in close to tell a joke. Harold is merry and Edith pensive. Gytha just to the left of Tostig smiles that taut smile of the mother who has lost two sons and has two more who care nothing for the lives they risk.

Harold's children now swarm their father, the boys and girls delighted at the tales and their hero father. As the night wears on, Leofwyn slumps first, then Edwin, and as time comes for the first sleep, the carls drag their lords to their beds while the rest bed down where they may. Harold wakes at midnight and nuzzles Edith. It is time again for them to be close and she takes him without a murmur.

* * *

Harold emerges fresh from his chamber at mid-morning. He summons the bleary pack to ride to his house, his father's house. Leofwyn is paying the Housecarls, all in various states of dishevelment, from the king's purse. Soon the spoils from the raid will come to Bosham and they will divide again. Edward will have his share. He grins at the accounting to come.

"Father," says Godwin, "five ships, is that really all?"

"More would have caused a stir, and it's hard to manage a larger raid in the night. Gruffyd never expected us to come. Not all the way from Bristol."

The boys don't yet understand, perhaps Magnus, so cunning already, so eager to be part of the action, would understand at their age.

"To horse, family, let's ride to Bosham while we can make it before dusk."

The servants gather and help the family organize their things while Harold preps his guard for the journey to Bosham. They walk to the stables, Harold's arm around his wife and the sleuth clucking around them. Now the weariness, the final push. They mount and head out at a clip, pushing on to sanctuary, to the home of his forefathers. They push on out of the gate, away from Edward and Edward free of the Godwins, such a place is England to place the dragon at the door of the King. Through the streets of Winchester, people waving and cheering at Harold and Leofwyn. The heroes grin at the throng as they go through the gate, as Edward and Tostig watch from the Solar.

"Your brother," says Edward admiringly, "could take the throne in a day."

"No Lord, and nor would our father have. Grandfather… perhaps. Harold loves what he is—what he was not born to be but what he got through Swein's intemperance. Forgive me lord, but you are lucky to have him—he will always serve you loyally."

"And you are not jealous, Tosty?"

"Jealous, no Lord, not at all. My wife, my Church, my king's favour and my brother's strong hand. All is well."

"Well, that is good, he has it easy in Wessex that one, and you would do well to remember how you brought the North to heel. To York, then, Tosty?"

"To York, my king," Tostig nods his head.

*   *   *

The group rides down with their guard past the sheep and cattle grazing lazily under the grey sky. Off in the near distance the squat church built by Godwin marks their destination. The men begin to slump in their saddles, and the children are saddle sore but careful not to moan in front of the great man, lest their grandmother's stare freeze them. A large palisade hides the great hall and the family hall, as longships patrol the waters and housecarls guard the grounds at all hours. Harold kicks his horse to a canter. Godgifu, heavily pregnant, sways a little and her husband restrains the urge to follow his brother and holds her arm. They are home. Mother Gytha breaks a rare smile as they approach the church, to pay their respects to Godwin and grandfather Wulfnoth, famous at sea, and so popular he divided a fleet at sea. They approach the graveyard and dismount. Harold and Leofwyn go first, and kneel beside the grave of their father, their mother follows and then the boys, each murmuring a short prayer. The old man taught him the sea and command of fleets; how to clear a deck of men and jump free of a sinking boat. His disgrace he avenged by turning on Aethelred's ships. The tides and tithes he learned from this man, who seemed never to see in Swein the darkness that was to devour him. Swein, buried in a far-off land and still his mother mourns him. Swein the heir – what would become of England with him as Earl? What would have become of the family?

"Mor," Harold says to Mother Gytha, "Vorse hjem er dit at styre." Our home is yours to manage.

"Ja, søn, og du er min at kommandere rundt," she smiled. You are mine to command.

"Come then family, let mother tell us what is what and let me rest awhile and not think of anything other than you and my goshawks."

They walk across the boardwalk from the church to the hall, the sea a constant presence in the near distance; here, the water of the inlet lapping against the quay where the longboats beat softly against the wooden platforms. It is so close to perfect here, the settlement sheltered by water and land around them making attack so impractical they barely need the walls of the palisade. Few places to beach boats and only one side abutting the land, it would take planning and patience to assault, by which time the inhabitants could travers the waters in three directions. Down past the verdant Thorney island and the Witterings through the natural harbour between them and Hayling, a ship could come in no time to Portsmouth and Southampton to the West. It is in this region that England's Southern fleet assembles, and where Harold influences most. Small, thatched dwellings ring the hall and the gulls wheel about their heads. The ground is often wet underfoot, so the halls are raised on stilts and the pathways made of wood and stone.

They trudge on to the hall, all the release of war and raids planning and politics sending the brothers' bodies into an early if temporary infirmity. Harold sways slightly and his men look away. Time for a bath and a pretty thrall to wash them down. They part ways with the women and children and move to the bathhouse. Both men slip into the hot water and lie back. Shapes coming out of the shadows, arms, knives, screams, a hasty thrust. A woman screaming, a child, bodies dismembered. Men screaming, choking. Fire. Sound of an axe through air. Through flesh, striking bone. Jarring. The beach, running. The old man. A hasty shield wall. Fire. That old woman's face. The pity of it. Guts. Wet floor and wet hands. The taste of blood. No feeling. Just flames and the sound of the axe against flesh. Harold sinks down as the thralls wash them and knead them. The urge to move, to get up, out, takes him. He forces it down. Leofwyn beside him in the next tub, eyes empty. He gets up urgently and the girl waits for him to sit. She kneads his shoulders and strokes his hair. Puts her face to his face and holds him. He sinks down again as she washes the grime and the sweat from him. He sinks into slumber, the ghosts and the horrors upon him washing away with her every stroke. To be empty again for a while.

* * *

Harold wakes with a start like a giant has breathed through him. He reaches up, out; he starts up and cannot rest, rises and reaches for a weapon. It is a ghost. He pulls his breeches on; Edith is sleeping still. He walks and the servants are beginning to stir between the two sleeps. He hardly sees them/ They nod to him. They have seen this and seen this. He grabs a cloak from the door and walks away towards land, bangs on the big gate to leave. He walks, the air is cool and damp through his bones. It is not fully dark, the stars and the moon light the way, but he walks like a man on a rope, further and further from shore, into the fields and meadows, across pathways not feeling a stone or thorn. Out, out, past the shepherds looking quizzically at him and the cattle paying no heed.

* * *

He wakes with Wulfric squatting over him grinning.

"Off on your travels again, Harold?"

"I fancied a walk during the watch."

"Hereward has a horse for you." Hereward is leaning against a tree. "Here's me thinking I'd get a good night's sleep tonight."

Harold grins and looks at his bare feet. He starts picking at the debris and the thorns.

"Boots, lord?" He nods and sits up. "I confessed in the chapel yesterday; it took a weight off." Wulfric seems at ease as he places his hand on his Lord's shoulder.

"You sound like Tostig."

"You should try it sometime. Even a man like you could do with sitting still and playing dice at watch."

Leofwyn rides up. He looks refreshed.

"Where to Harold? A raid on Malcom today?" Harold laughs heartily and rubs his head.

"Home, Wyn. I'm hungry. Then let's go hawking. Take the boys out." Leofwyn nods as Harold pulls his boots on. "That was a good sleep."

"Always good to be out in nature, lord. Good for the soul," says Wulfric.

The four men ride the six miles back to Bosham through the fields and the trees. His people smile and wave at their lord.

"Heavy night there, Earl Harold," one farmer pipes up. Harold grins.

"You'll never shake your youth Harold," Leofwyn smiles. Just as well. 'Harold the Mad' is not a moniker he will wear lightly.

* * *

That morning the eat breakfast in the family hall. The great crossbeams above them are carved with dragons and sea beasts, and light shines through the high windows down onto them. Tapestries of hunting and seafaring in the English style hang against the walls along with the shields and weapons of allies and enemies from generations. He will hang Gryffud's sword here, Olaf having snatched it from the King's hall; he was paid handsomely for the gesture, The servants busy serving food prepared in the kitchen, while the warriors eat in the great hall, their occasional laughter breaking through the quiet. They are so close to the sea, the waves are a constant presence, and the salt air soothes the earl. Soon it will be time to greet the villagers and spend some time with the men.

Gytha looks at her son with concern and shakes her head. She clucks at the servants as they bring the stews and bread. Harold calls for more bacon and smiles at his family. Edith is used to him, she rises and kisses him tenderly on the cheek and he smiles the smile of a man who chose his woman, and whose woman gave herself to him willingly. Second son, the warrior, the one to risk and given license to choose.

"It would be nice to have uncle Gyrth here too, father," Godwin says. Uncle Gyrth bringing joy to the table with his hearty laugh.

"And Tostig, too," says mother. They all shrug.

"We'll say a prayer, then, mor," says Leofwyn and bows his head miming a prayer. The children laugh. Gytha cuts it short with an ice-cold stare. No mention of Wulfstan, the shame of his being hostage weighs heavily on the men.

"Boys, we are going hawking."

"Me too," states Magnus flatly.

"Oh really?" His father asks.

"Really." No arguing, then.

"What about me?" His daughter asks.

"Learn to bake and sew," laughs Harold. She throws a hunk of bread at him. Gytha smacks her hard on the shoulder.

"Let her go too, Harold, or give her a sister."

"That last I have been working at the last few nights," he says, and Godgifu chokes on her soup, suppressing a laugh. "Fine, young Gytha, you can come and watch your brothers." She scowls and bows her head. Mother shakes her head at these boys.

"You never change, either of you."

"Sådan er vi bare, mor." It's our way.

"You could always visit Tostig in the North, Mother." Edith says mildly. Harold places his hand on his wife's arm. Gytha straightens her tall hard body.

"He's a good boy, that Tostig," says Leofwyn, and the family bow their heads smirking into their chests.

"Right, then," says Harold. "Let's get those hawks and find some rabbits. Would you put some bacon and bread in a sack for us, Magnus?" The old servant nods with a smile and has a skin of water and ale brought besides.

Edith meets her mother-in-law's eyes mildly. Gytha folds her arms and barks an order at a thrall to clear the table.

*   *   *

"Are we really descended from a bear," Magnus asks, as they trot along the fields towards a small hill North from Bosham.

"That would have been a painful night for your great grandmother," laughs Harold, his goshawk hooded and perched on his wrist. Gytha blushes.

"A bear as large as Goliath," says Leofwyn, "See how your father can lift a man. You should see him fight, too, boys…Gytha…He can swipe a man clean off the face of the earth."

"Uncle Wyn, are you a good fighter too?"

"The best," says Harold, "And utterly without fear. He charged a shield wall at Rhuddlan." Leofwyn beams at his brother's compliment.

"Let us show the lads the shield wall tomorrow, Lord," Olaf says from the back.

"I'll join you," Harold nods, "The land and then the sea, boys. We have a month together. Let's make the most of it."

"Edmund puked last time we were in a ship," Godwin smirks.

"Then Edmund will learn to sail while puking," his father laughs.

"Where is Oswald, anyway," asks the Earl.

"Now let's have a good think together, Lord, and we'll get right back to you on that one." The men laugh.

"Alfred will have his balls if he finds out," says Hereward.

"A thousand husbands will venerate him and proclaim miracles at the grave of St Alfred if he does," laughs Hereward.

They ride on to Bow Hill, Magnus and another servant riding roughly behind on a cart with their lunch. Two handlers manage a further two hawks, perched and tied carefully to a specially made saddle. The housecarls suddenly ride on ahead, the five men spreading out across the fields, careful to avoid farmers and travellers. They sweep up over the hill in their leather tunics and bright blue shirts, bows slung across their backs and their axes sheathed by their saddles. There are few outlaws here, but the protocol is always the same. The family ride up leisurely and Harold begins his sermon.

"The goshawk is a hard bird to train, but the best in catching prey," The children gather. Gytha is already bored. "He unhoods his hawk, the great glove on his left hand protecting him from the claws. The bird's head twitches left and right, stunned by the daylight. "This is my bird. You boys will have to accept that those two are the handlers' birds. When you release them," he pauses to untie the hawk with his right hand, "they will return to their masters." He flicks his wrist and the bird takes flight. As a group they follow the goshawk as it beats its wings into the air and begins to circle. There are some scattered clouds on this grey morning, but they can see for miles around. "Look there! See it circle. It can spot its prey from miles away. Look at it move, if only man could have such wings. It hangs in the air for a moment and then dives. Magnus whoops. It disappears from view, then up it comes and beats its wings back to its master, within moments it is back, a dead kit in its beak. He places the hawk on the pommel of his saddle and lets it eat a little. The children clap, they have heard this a hundred times but today there is more. "Today, you boys will have a chance to hunt with a hawk. Godwin, Edmund, go get a glove each from the cart. Yes there. On your left-hand Edmund. Wyn you're up next. Aethelstan, Arnulf, help them tie the gloves, there. Ok boys."

"What about me?" Magnus is hurt.

"You? Well, let's see." Harold dismounts and goes to the cart. He fetches a smaller glove and walks over to his youngest son, taking his hand roughly and putting the glove on. "Try that and wave your arm around." The boy hangs his head. Harold walks to his horse and shifts the hawk onto his own glove. Kneeling down he gently transfers the bird to his boy's hand and props it as it sags under the unexpected weight. "Heavy, no?" The boy nods gratefully. Harold pumps his hand under the boy's left arm and the goshawk flies up and swoops around the sky. Leofwyn's hawk moves quickly into its own space and dives before the competition can react.

"There," says Harold, "Let's see what he can do for you, Magnus." The boy straightens his back proudly and watches the hawk as it hovers and dives again. Now the others' hawks are up in the air, and they shout and laugh at their movements. Harold stands and nods to his brother, whose own hawk returns with a small snake.

"Now that's a sign," says Leofwyn.

"I'll take that as one too," says Harold. Mercia.

The other hawks return to their handlers and the older boys trudge up to gawp at the birds feeding on their prey.

The day passes like this, the boredom disappeared now the children have a role. They eat their lunch in the open fields and Harold recounts his time in Flanders fighting for the Holy Roman Emperor against Baldwin. Even the Housecarls are silent as he flatly tells the stories of his naval battles and raids.

"But father, wasn't grandfather exiled to Flanders? Why would you fight against Baldwin?"

"Why do men fight at all? It was my king's command, and I fought at his will."

"It's why your father and I spent our exile in Ireland," says Leofwyn, "Your grandfather was against the expedition, but your father went anyway."

"I was seventeen, and at my King's mercy."

"Seventeen father," Magnus gaped.

"Yes. Exactly that."

"Seventeen and clearing a ship's deck like a man possessed, so Alfred tells us," Wulfric smiles admiringly at his Earl.

"But uncle Tostig married Aunt Judith," says Gytha screwing her face up.

"Exactly. And I did not. I got your mother instead." He lies back in the grass and stares up at the heavens.

"Did Count Baldwin forgive you?"

"Forgive? He took his licks and now we can feast together."

"Thanks to father," Leofwyn chastises gently.

"And a large chest of gold," laughs Harold. "Time to go, my sleuth. Let's gather ourselves and head back to mother."

"What then, Earl," asks Wulfric pointedly.

"Oh, I'll see the priest tomorrow."

"Right, then."

"Another restful night for me then," says Hereward.

"There's always Flanders, Hereward. I brought you back from exile for your axe not your tongue."

"I'm just fine under you, Lord."

"Well then."

They ride back to Bosham with Olaf shaking his head at Hereward. Leofwyn grins at the men.

"Olaf, see that you have a word with our Oswald. And keep it away from Alfred for God's sake."

"Yes Jarl Harold."

*   *   *

The next day the warriors assemble in full armour. Godwin and Edmund have been similarly dressed and are arrayed before the men.

"Wall," Harold commands. Then to the boys, "Break it."

They gape at him in their youth.

"Break it."

Terrified, Godwin runs and stops dead at a Norman shield. He bangs his own, smaller shield against the wall. Then he pushes. Edmund comes up and tries his luck. They push harder, their feet digging into the earth. After a short while they give up.

"Why did you stop? I told you to break it."

They turn around and look at their father's grim face. They try again. Local lads in their dirty windings and coarse breeches lean against the haystacks smirking at their Earl's sons' humiliation.

"Harder."

They push, as if for an age, little Magnus staring at them in contempt.

"Forward." Harold shouts, and the line moves a step forward and the boys tumble.

Edith is standing at a distance with her mother-in-law, fist against her mouth.

"When it was Swein and Harold, I thought one or both of them would die," Gytha says, squeezing Edith's arm. "Godwin was a harder man than Harold."

"Perhaps that's why Swein was the way he was." Gytha smarts as if the accusation was from nowhere.

"It is why Harold is the way he is." They lapse back into habitual silence as the trial continues.

He makes them repeat their charge until they are sweat soaked even in this cool spring morning. Against the sound of shield upon shield the waves slap against the shore and the gulls wheel and cry. When the sun has climbed a few steps higher the boys are defeated. Harold drags them up by their mail shirts and hauls them back.

"Watch." He braces his shield against his arm and charges the wall at its weakest point between two shields. The shields move back inches, but the wall stands. He does it again.

"Wyn!" Leofwyn charges a horse against the wall. It shifts slightly and a man groans. Leofwyn manages to keep his balance and trots his horse back.

"See?" Their father ushes the boy forward. "These men will stand for hours. They will never budge. We train the fyrd to be like them. The simplest of formations – a human wall. But watch now. Olaf, Cyneweard, Harald, Asbjorn, Ivar. Forward." The big men wielding axes swing them over the heads of the shield wall, arcing then motioning to pull a man. "Archers!" Men fire dummy arrows over the wall. Harold motions for the wall to part and walks the boys around. "This is how we stand and fight – integrated arms – wall, axemen, archers. We never break the line, and we never stop pushing. You gave up too quickly."

The boys nod. The local lads have stopped laughing as Harold motions to the largest of them. He orders shields and has them stand with the warriors. "Now then you lads. Let's see you stand fast." He takes a few steps back and charges at one of them. The boy goes down and Harold breaks through. He kicks the boy hard as he goes across.

"Here I am, lads. A Welsh warrior among you thrashing the archers and his friends following through. All because this cocky shit couldn't hold his ground." The lad is writhing on the ground, Harold pays it no mind and lets his friends pick him up and take him off to his home. Older men now have trickled in and raise their hands. Harold lets them stand in the wall and has his housecarls test the formations. He has his boys stand and get knocked over again and again. They sit on the floor defeated.

"This is how we get strong, boys. We lift stones. We split logs. We row like sailors and heave ships bodily out to sea. We wrestle men and we run in our mail shirts. Today was the beginning of your journey to manhood. You didn't cry, which is good. But you need more fight. And you need more grit. You boys," motioning to the youths stood around. "Come and look at your future Lords. They took their licks and suffered in front of their men. And they will take their licks again and again until they are stones and timbers. And they will lead men like you and you will learn to obey and respect them because like me they are harder and more unforgiving than any other man. Get stronger and learn your role in battle. To stand fast and obey."

The youths nod as their fathers and elders look away awkwardly. The older men have done well today. Seasoned by practice they will knock their lads around until they learn. Harold's face is grim.

"Your earl is a hair's breadth from ripping off your arms lads," Leofwyn chastises as he walks the youths away.

"Boys," Harold pulls his sons to him in a hug. "I leave you in the care of Alfred, he will train you and I will test you. And he will show you no mercy. The we will teach you more about the sea. War is coming and you will learn that too." Godwin stands tall and removes his helmet. He stares his father in the eye and nods. Edmund is slower but nods his head in resignation. Young Magnus surveys his brothers critically before hauling a stone at one of the local boys. The yelp pleases him, and he walks up and down the line of warriors like a king.

"And you, Magnus, are coming fishing." The boy grins and puts his hand into his father's large paw.

Harold calls for a horse and orders the villagers and priests to gather.

"I Harold, Earl of Essex, in the name of our King, Edward, call upon the free and able men of Essex to assemble under the law of the Fyrd. To practice arms and be ready for war within the month. And I call on the sailors of Wessex, merchants and warriors to assemble under my brother's orders at Southampton and Bristol in readiness for war. Priests, write this down and have men ride to every Shire Reeve and Thegn with my orders, save Cornwall; those men may choose to come or not."

There are scattered cheers and fire in the eyes of his warriors.

This night will be spent in the great hall with half his men, while the rest patrol. They will switch the next night. For now, they clean their armour and mother the boys, bruised and half crippled by their entry into the world of men.

* * *

Harold is seated at the head of his table in the large hall. The men are chanting and happy. So many meats and fish are laid before them and the promise of their share of treasure is a source of joyful planning of their futures. Godwin and Edmund sit among the men in their best blue and green tunics. Magnus is allowed at the head table by his uncle's side. They will pass the next week in this way, training by day and feasting all night. The wounds heal and the bodies begin to return to the power and grace they began with. Lands are disbursed close to Winchester and Bosham so the men may profit while performing their duties. To Leofwyn, contiguous lands on the border with Mercia, enough income for a family and an Ealdorman's status promised after the war; he is cheered for a long time, this brother to them all. Next the boys are hauled onto the table and hailed by their new brothers. One evening Olaf is told to sit with the other Norwegians, much to the amusement of the Danes and English. He hurls his drinking horn in mock disgust and sits alone on a chair on top of his table daring any man to knock him off. There is wrestling, jibing and singing but no scores are settled here, the brotherhood is secure, and every man will have his share. Even the sailors from Rhuddlan are brought in to be hailed by their comrades. One particularly drunken night the men began to chant:

"Hail Harold, King of Wessex." Harold feels the accolade wash over him like a warm wave before he catches himself and rises quickly with his hand on his head. He raises both hands.

"For the love of England and your Earl stop this. We are at war."

The men are silenced.

"But we can take the King of Wales's crown!" They cheer and thump the table.

"With his head still in it!" one of the warriors calls out. They all cheer again.

"I pray the king doesn't hear of this," Harold mutters to Leofwyn as he sits down again.

"That's the first prayer you've said in a while, brother. I'm starting to like the change in you." They laugh.

After four nights spent feasting and days spent playing war, Harold will tour the village and its environs, greeting the locals and sharing tales of their youths. Men and women flock to him in the villages around, the tales of his raid growing taller by the day. The browns and blacks of their clothes contrast his bright red tunic and blue breeches. Groomed with his blond hair falling over his forehead, his face not yet salt cured yet the creases in his eyes growing deeper. Still strong, perhaps stronger than his youth, the older men look at him proudly as a thegn and son of the same earth as their sons. Quick to laugh with them, grasp shoulders, and slow to temper outside of the war machine and court, he is an ealdorman again, at ease among his folk. He walks with his hounds brushing his legs and his brother by his side, watchful and pleasant with his long-combed hair and cropped moustache framing a pleasant sun-tanned face with eyes that move between warmth and emptiness.

Crowds and local thegns and reeves greet the heroes as they tour the walled town of Chichester. As usual the books are turned over, much to the amazement of the administrators who expected more of a celebratory visits, and Harold and his brother pore through the incomes and expenditures, marking discrepancies and questioning the reeve and local merchants. They visit the market and buy at random with smiles, haggling half-heartedly and loading their servants up with unnecessary wares. Town this this are suffocating, the stench and the crush of people in gridlocked streets. Far preferable, the villages like Fishbourne, Appledram and Donnington. The folk all getting their spits ready and roasting meats for their lord, the open fields and farm smells recalling his youth, ale barrels wheeled out and instruments coming out. There is dancing after the work is done and the Earl joins in in his own way, wheeling girls around while his brother, cocksure, chats up the girls. Next the men exhort him to feats of strength, stones are dragged up and men again organize into teams. Backs are thrown and Harold hauls a large stone round the sheep enclosure of Fishbourne. Another man, Wiglaf manages a quarter turn more, and Harold, delighted, hands him coins from his own purse. As the week wears on, Harold is restless.

"Wyn, it's time to call up the Fyrd at sea, have men sent to the four corners – we will raid from the South to make a point. For now, stay in Southampton and organize things from there. We will shoot for a month. Give leeway to men in the North to raid if they will; time will be wasted with the trip down. We will maintain coherence of the fleet. Remember, everything is coming from the King's purse so, as usual, keep a careful record." Leofwyn rolls his eyes.

"I need to say it."

"And you might visit Father Dunstan."

"Fine, I'll go. I have a tale to tell."

The next morning Harold makes his way across the wooden bridge, to the stone church, where he is greeted by Father Dunstan, tall and lean, his hands showing a scribe's work.

"Earl Harold, such a surprise to see you on a day other than Sunday."

"I'm here for my confession."

The priest looks him in the eye.

"Clear your day father."

"Come, my son, my ear and God's are yours."

Harold sits before the priest and begins "I have sinned in words, thought and deed."

The day progresses, and towards Terce, the priest places his hands on Harold's shoulders, his eyes moist with tears.

"What's the penance?"

"Bless you Harold. Fund the maintenance of Selsey."

"But I have killed, I have plotted other men's deaths, I have thought ill of my lord and taken slaves."

"For England, Harold. You have done your duty. Bless you, Lord. Bless you."

Wulfric is waiting outside the thick oak doors.

"How do you feel, lord?"

"Like I just entertained a priest with tales for half the day."

"I may have to visit the holy land at some point."

"Wulfric, what the fuck do you do behind my back?"

"Everything in your service lord. Mostly," the large, swarthy man smirks.

"And where is Oswald," he has been missing for days.

"In a land dispute, lord. Alfred was aware."

"A land dispute? And why am I not aware of this?"

"Too petty for your ears lord. Feeling better anyway?"

"A bit I suppose, but I do wonder how our faith accepts a warrior's life."

"I bring not peace but the sword, lord."

"Well then."

"Harold?"

Harold shakes his head and walks back across the causeway to the privy.

* * *

In the walled and gird-lined port city of Southampton, Leofwyn is organizing the call up of the sea-Fyrd from the great hall. He has thegns, merchants and captains assembled. Riders have been provisioned and sent to the major ports already with letters stamped with Edward's seal. Leaders have been summoned from the coastal areas of Wessex and the captains of the Bosham fleet are present. Leofwyn is briefing the men on their course of action. One captain, a middling height man called Edmund, raises his hand among the assembled throng mid-speech.

"Yes," Leofwyn grimaces at the interruption.

"First, congratulations on becoming a father, a boy is it. That's something to leave behind. What about the security of the coast when we are at war? We're leaving ourselves open to raiders."

"Earl Harold has called for sixty to one hundred ships. We can accommodate the usual coast guard." Another raises his hand.

"Yes?"

"But what happens when we're done raiding? Where does it end?"

"You drop us off at the assigned point and you go home. Lads, this is easy. We're not even going to raid the whole of Wales. The goal is to show the Welsh how weak Gryffud is."

"If he'd been caught in the first place we wouldn't have to do this," another man shouted. There is silence. This was not Harold they were talking to.

"Well then, you go ahead and destroy the Welsh capital with a handful of ships."

"We will have a navy, where we had a small group. We will have an army raiding on land while we harry the coast. And we will give the Welsh a choice — Gruffyd or barren fields." There are nods of approval. "Wessex…England…will be safe and each of you will get a share of the spoils."

"And take some Welsh girls home!"

"About that." There are groans. "We have been…admonished by the King, and Bishop Wulfstan, and the holy see…No slaves. No killing of children. No rape."

"But killing everyone else is fine?" There is laughter.

"I thought this would be good business for Earl Harold," a thegn, face pockmarked and scarred says.

"It will be good business for Wessex, and it will pay for itself. It's also a national call out, so it's even better for…our purse. Now, any more questions about why we're doing this, or can we get back to how?"

* * *

Tostig has ridden North to York, joined by Gyrth and Morcar. Rain comes down, making their woollen cloaks stink. Gyrth is smiling as usual; his face broader and more pleasant than Tostig's refined features. He will accompany them as far as Stamford where he will break off to Tamworth to ensure the Mercian fyrd is being assembled. His thegns are beginning the call out for provisions in East Anglia.

"So, Morcar, I suppose you're our hostage now."

"Well, since my sister is home, you could argue that I have no reason to help Gruffyd in any way."

"You seem like a good sort. I'd have a hard time cutting your head off if your father betrays us," Gyrth grins at Morcar, his housecarls miming various forms of death from their horses.

They are three hundred strong, plus baggage hung on spare horses to quicken their journey. They will be able to requisition supplies from Mercia and station themselves along the route.

"Gyrth, when will the east Anglian fyrd be ready to assemble at Tamworth?" Tostig asks, smiling faintly at the banter.

"For the third time, brother, they will be at Tamworth in twenty days. You have thirty total before they start to cause trouble so make haste and pray your own house is in order."

"Sorry brother, I'm fretting on my own behalf." Gyrth pays him a sympathetic nod.

"It's a bad roll of the dice for sure, brother, you're stuck between two bears and there's no taming either of them."

"I do as my king commands."

"That man changes his mind every Tuesday, if he orders you in one direction one day, you'll be heading in the opposite direction the next." The warriors around him laugh heartily.

"Hush brother, we have had peace among our kingdom for twenty years thanks to Edward."

"Perhaps as a result of your family running most of it," smiles Morcar.

"That, my new friend, is a truth indeed. Now Morcar, are you coming with me or is Tostig intent on forcing you to witness the puzzle that is Northumbria?"

"He'll come North with me," Tostig interrupts.

"I've always wanted to see York, and from what I hear, your brother has done more than any other to tame that Northern bear."

"It was best left as it was, with its own rules and its own peace. No fault of yours brother, you have done well despite its nature."

"There is still peace for the most part. Especially at York, I am fond of it, and the people are loyal."

"Harold always says you were given the worst of the kingdom because the king had the most faith in you. And yet he wants you at court all the time."

"I am favoured, I know this."

"I'd say you're damned but that's just me. Brother, be proud: you were a burning flame of justice for five years – that's an eternity up there. Half-Dane or no, you can't change a man's nature. Or a region's."

"Sometimes, Gyrth, it's best to stop talking."

"Earl Gyrth will be talking in his grave," laughs one of the warriors, and even Tostig laughs, his unlined eyes creasing.

They traipse on through the sodden land, Gyrth pointing out landmarks and inventing tales, heckling the odd traveller on Ermine street.

At Stamford they dismount and spend the evening talking of their father with their new friend, of Godwin's rise after Wulfnoth's rebellion. And disfavour.

"I'm sure," says Tostig bemused at fate, "if our grandfather had not fled Athelred's fleet with twenty ships, we would not be where we are. We'd be sons of a thegn in Sussex, kicking our heels and ploughing the fields."

"I think, brother, if the eighty chasing him had not been wrecked we may not be here at all."

"Cnut," says Morcar.

"Yes," says Tostig, "that wrecked fleet opened the door for Cnut to come. God's will I suppose."

"Men followed Wulfnoth," says Morcar.

"Yes they loved him, just as they love Harold."

"They love Harold more; what he has done for England brother, what he still does. Grandfather made a big mess for England. Harold has kept us safe."

"Your grandfather didn't make the weather."

"That is true. Gyrth—I would like to visit the shrine of Our Lady of Walsingham."

"You are welcome any time brother. It's just a fucking hut that Richeldis woman had built and now all the pious are running around calling it an act of god. I have to go and act amazed and humbled at a miracle of bad carpentry instead of praying at an actual saint's reliquary."

"Still, they say she is a holy woman."

"I'll tell you one thing."

"What's that?"

"She doesn't wash frequently." Morcar laughs heartily at Gyrth.

"It's our father's fault, Morcar: only Tostig and Wulfstan really took to Church. Not that I don't pray, I…well…we were raised to serve our country and God practically and with common sense."

"Edward favoured me, that is true and brought me closer to God."

"You did walk a bit funny for a while," Gyrth grins at Morcar.

"I think Edward is not that way."

"Then why is our sister still a virgin?"

"I think, perhaps. He swore an oath never to bed the daughter of Godwin when he forced the marriage."

"So, he cut off his nose to spite father."

"Perhaps not his nose," says Morcar and he and Gyrth wipe tears from their eyes when they are done laughing.

"Let's pay the King the respect he is due."

"We are just concerned over the succession, brother, no offense meant."

Tostig stares into the fire, his eyes absent.

"Tostig you're doing the fire thing."

"What fire thing," Morcar asked.

"When father stared into the fire, we knew to be quiet. He'd stare for an eternity."

"And what did he see?"

"Perhaps we should go to bed," says Tostig, shaking himself to.

Gyrth stretched and rises first from the old oak chair he is sprawled in, his large frame stiff from the ride.

"I'll be off at dawn brother. Make haste – we don't want an army of bored men tearing up the countryside this side of the border."

"Sleep well, Gyrth. I'll see you soon."

*   *   *

The next day, Tostig, Morcar and one hundred housecarls, sundry servants and two priests make the journey north. They leave Gyrth sleeping while his men busy themselves preparing for their journey West. The journey remains damp, yet Morcar is cheerful.

"I hope I can fight beside you, Tostig, I have heard of your battles in the North."

"Mostly skirmishes, hardly at my brother's level."

"Still, you have a reputation."

"And it would be less overwhelming than fighting at Harold's side."

"It would be a better entry into warfare at your side. Mercia traditionally fought the Welsh, but I've had no opportunity after father's…peacemaking."

Tostig nods. A slight smile appears on his face.

"That's a fine way of putting it."

Ermine street, well-travelled, occasionally maintained, leads the band up to Lincoln, where they rest. The ride West to Gainsborough to avoid the unreliable ferry and cross the Humber. After three days of sodden riding, they arrive at the great timber gates of York. Tostig's arrival, to Morcar's open surprise, is greeted with friendly deference by the people. The reeve and thegns ride out to meet their earl with open affection. Men of Danish and English extraction all, they greet him as an older brother and are quick to bring news of the North. Chief among them Copsig, a tall and reedy man who quickens his horse's pace to reach his lord.

"Copsig, what news," the Earl greets his lieutenant warmly, reaching his hand out quickly.

"It's been too long, lord, too long. More trouble from Hundwine and his gang in the far North. They are taking cattle as payment for their losses to Scottish raids. The raids themselves have been fewer, perhaps due to Malcom's influence, although the weather has been bad. My lands have been affected too, Tostig, and I ask for leave once you're settled to deal with the issue."

"When we are back from Wales, Copsig, you will have your leave."

With Copsig are the Reeve Stanboda, and two thegns, Bradan and Athelgar. Copsig nods, resigned.

"We received the King's orders, Lord. And who leads this expedition?"

"I'll lead the land army while Harold takes the navy. Then he will land, and we will converge on the Welsh strongholds."

'Your brother is quite the risk taker," laughs Stanboda, "His raid is the talk of Northumbria. We have called out the fyrd, lord. There is some resistance in the far North, but we will have at least a thousand. Plus, your Housecarls."

"We have the Mercians, East Anglians and some men from Wessex under Harold's chief, Alfred. It will be enough – some four thousand five hundred to Harold's force of fifteen hundred. We are calling men from Deira and Bernicia yes?"

"Of course, Earl, and even some troublemakers from the border."

"It would be good to have Hundwine and others send men to build some unity." The men look astonished.

"We could try, but it would be easier to get men from Malcom," Aethelgar, stout ealdorman demurs. His lined face betrays a hint of pity.

"Yes, perhaps you're right."

As they ride to the Earl's hall, he tells them of the plan to meet Gyrth at Tamworth and then ride the route of Watling street until they cross the border.

"Your wife, lord?"

"She is staying in Winchester. This is a short trip, Copsig, we will need to make haste and ensure there is no trouble."

"All is well in York, Lord."

"Yes, but the rest. We will ride out tomorrow together and supervise the fyrd. Make sure my housecarls are assembled – we will divide them in two. A bodyguard and the rest to remain here."

"And what am I to do?" Morcar has been looking around at the mix of Nordic and English houses with delight.

"You can come tomorrow, and we will see after then, my friend."

After bathing and changing into a deep blue tunic, Tostig heads to St Peter's for prayers with his men. They will invite Bishop Ealdred for the evening meal and talk long into the night about ecclesiastical matters. The Bishop promises to ride with the army as far as the border, and perhaps beyond, his health permitting. The next day they ride North to assemble the fyrd.

"I'm mindful of my brother Gyrth's words," Tostig remarks to Morcar as they ride through the fields beyond York's protective embrace. "We can't afford a rabble causing trouble in Mercia."

"And what of the North, Tostig, will raising the Fyrd cause further trouble?"

"I hope not, but we must follow the King's will. How am I to lead an army without providing my share? We must hope that Hundewine, Arnulf, and Harald Thorkilsonn don't take advantage. But it is a partial call-out. We shall leave a garrison behind."

"So, York will be safe."

"York will always be provided for."

Again, Aethelgar shakes his head as they ride.

"Trouble, Aethelgar," asks Tostig?

"Here, Tostig, there is always trouble, never peace. Just the weight of the King's yoke on the northern cash cow."

Tostig remains silent, caught between two bears.

*   *   *

They ride out, the housecarls surrounding their Lord and his retinue. As usual, men are sent out ahead in the drizzle to scout out the landscape. At Easingwold, they encounter polite acknowledgement as the people come out for a rare glimpse of their Earl. Tostig returns their greetings behind a wall of mounted men. The fyrd is gathering here. Men lugging spears and hand axes, a rare sword is wrapped against the rain. Ad hoc practices are occurring, and he pauses to watch a half-hearted charge in the mud. Men are already complaining about the mud and women shake their heads while others weep in advance of their men traveling so far from home for a foreign king.

"They're good for a brawl," Morcar laughs at the haphazard attempts to form a fighting band.

"That's basically what we need them for; that and staying tight together until they're told to move. You there, Arnulf, you're thegn here. Have these men form up and see how long they can stick together. We leave in a week so make sure every man can march and carry his load."

He turns to Copsig.

"Copsig, how are our supplies? We will need to run our lines down to Tamworth with the army."

"We are still procuring, Lord. It's just past sowing season and the lambs have come so it's a tricky time."

"We have granaries and stores, cheese and vegetables, Copsig. I want enough to feed us until we reach the border. Then we will take what we need." He throws him a bag of gold. "Take one fifth from the area around here and leave the far North be. We don't need more trouble. Say 30 cows or equivalent meat. Two hundred sheep or the equivalent, two hundred sacks of grain and as many sturdy covered carts as you can muster."

Copsig nods and points to his men, beginning to open the bag.

"No, Copsig. You must go and ensure we have this done swiftly. We will have a band ride with the train within two days. Two days, Copsig. Then you will accompany us to Tamworth and then..." he raises his hand, "You may return to York."

Copsig nods and kicks his horse into a trot.

"That man seems sleepy," says Morcar quietly.

"He is capable, but a more energetic man might cause me trouble here. To Thirsk."

They ride on. As they reach Thirsk, they have the same scenes of gradual assembly, the same polite gestures. Here Tostig and then men dismount and have their horses fed. They will rest at the hall where Bradan is Thegn. He has some two hundred men mustering from the regions around. Here they get news of the North.

"As expected, Hundewine and the others have ignored the call," Arnulf seems unphased. "We will still get our headcount but there's talk in Richmond that the call out will encourage the far North to encroach."

"What do you recommend, Arnulf?"

"A show of support would be good, lord. Perhaps some housecarls stationed behind the walls to show readiness."

"Perhaps we can spare twenty from York."

"Twenty is a start."

"I need fifteen hundred men, not the entire region. We can send some up for the duration. The king will allow it."

"A third of the region gone," says Aethelgar.

"Not gone, Aethelgar, soaking up the border raids."

"An argument for another time, Tostig." Tostig, chillingly calm, looks at Aethelgar dead in the eye.

"Remember when I first came here, Aethelgar. A man does not change, he only rests that part of him that is not needed."

The men are silent around their lord.

Aethelgar nods.

"That Tostig I like."

Morcar grins.

"Well then, Tostig, you are a killer as much as your brother."

"Don't we know it," Arnulf laughs and claps his earl on the shoulder.

They set off in the dim morning light, up Dere street and past the old Roman fort of Catterick, where the odd farmer and his son walk or ride to meet their brothers in arms. Some men give hearty greetings, excited to be fighting; others scowl at the imposition, but still they come. They ride along the winding Swale up towards the rising dales and the timber palisade around the promontory of Richmond. Here they pause and send two riders ahead to check the temperature. Morcar sits, a half grin on his face.

"Yes, Morcar," Aethelgar says. "This is how things are."

"It is…what does Edward say…protocol. Even Harold does this in Wessex of all places," Tostig is unfazed by the Ealdorman's criticism.

"I have not spent much time with Harold outside of court, that is true."

The riders come back and nod to their lord who starts slowly up the winding path up towards the town. Inside, life is much as usual. Tostig shoots Copsig, who rode ahead the prior day, a hard look, the man visible cringes.

"Copsig."

"Lord, the men are assembling north of here."
"How many men and where are the provisions?"

"Coming."

"Coming."

"Yes, one day lord."

"One day's duration or one day, someday, Copsig."

"A day lord."

Tostig shunts his horse past a small crowd who have come to gawp at their prodigal Earl. An apple flies through the air and hits him on his shoulder. The immediate area falls silent. He turns his head to look towards a woman holding a basket of apples. She shakes her head frantically at him. He scans the area, and the crowd takes a step back as one. Tostig dismounts nimbly. The basket of apples falls to the floor. He walks over slowly. A man instinctively reaches for his dagger and Tostig moves quicker than his men and shoves the man so hard he crashes through three rows of people to the ground. He pushes his way through the crowd, grabs the dagger and stomps on the man's groin. He walks back slowly and inspects the dagger, his back turned. Then he looks at the woman.

"Pick them up."

Shaking so hard she can barely follow his orders, she picks the apples up. Next to her a small boy has wet himself.

"Was it you?" The boy nods, his face ashen.

"Well then. Rebellion starts young, here. If you had hit my face my wife would be very, very displeased" Pointing to the woman. "You missed one – pick it up and go and wash those apples clean. The street is filthy. Then he takes two steps back, waving his men off.

"You're taking my father away."

"And the king is taking me away from my son and wife. What am I to do? Throw some fruit? Clean yourself up, little man, it's a hard thing to watch a brave boy covered in piss." Then he looks out to the crowd, the tension easing at his mildness.

"The king called out the Fyrd, and yet, so close to York, I do not see the activity he ordered. You have three days to organize your men and have them start on their way. Food, arrows, bows, carts. All the things that have been requisitioned will go through this...man, Copsig. Get moving folks, we are at war."

"Why are we fighting some foreign foe, when the Scots are raiding?" One man, unperturbed by Tostig's reputation speaks up.

"Because the King orders it."

"This foreign king in a Southern Kingdom."

"Yes. And my brother Harold orders it so. And if you have a problem, I can have you brought South to Harold, and he can explain the entire reason for it while you row for three weeks on his ship. Or you can get a spear and do your duty."

"Then do your duty and secure our borders."

"First the Welsh and then the North. This I commit to. Three days, people. You have had four weeks or more. You, loudmouth. Go out the northern gate and assemble with the others. Once you're blooded in Wales, we can travel North together. Let's see if your arm is as strong as your mouth is loud." The people chuckle as the man stands alone in the crowd.

"Send me the bill for this man – I fear I may have made him a bullock," pointing at the overeager knife wielder. This time, laughter. "I am serious, though. Don't make me take your goods. There is enough bad blood in our lands." Danish and English eyes narrow.

They head out to inspect those men who have honoured the call-up.

* * *

So, the fyrd is mustered. The best carts mysteriously lose wheels or are lost altogether; farmers are caught hiding grain and butchers are ordered to remain outside their stores as the priests with their housecarl bodyguards assess the tithe. The only happy men are the blacksmiths and the wrights. Reshoeing horses and getting spears, axes and Saxon shields into shape. The long Norman shields of the housecarls have taken hold in the South and Midlands but still men prefer the old circular shape up here. The slow movement of wheels and men prodded on by warriors turns into a slog South as the few men from the far North trickle into the assembly point. Barrels of ale and spring water are given the lead, with the cured meat at the rear; now the housecarls will guard the train as much as their lord. There is the usual weeping and clinging of children to their fathers and brothers, but since news of Harold's victory, there is not much foreboding. The English are invading for once. Tostig and his fifteen hundred men, sundry priests, one Bishop, the Bishop's entourage, and a handful of loyal thegns and Ealdormen begin the traipse down to Tamworth, churning up the mud beside the Roman road.

* * *

Harold is fishing just out to sea with Magnus. The waves lap like a dog's tongue against the boat, big enough to fit ten men, but holding just four today. The sun hangs in the thin blue sky and slight clouds drift under a whisper of a wind. They have nets spread out and hanging off ropes from the stern, and Harold casts a line out, hooked with sundry parts of meat in the hope of catching lunch.

"Father, were you ever in trouble?"

"Trouble? Why, what did you do?"

"Nothing. You always seem to be in charge that's all."

"Oh, I'm not really in charge, Magnus – you'll learn, your grandmother rules the roost here, and at court I need to follow the king's orders – or perhaps act and hope he approves."

"But you're in charge here."

"Yes, in Wessex I am, but only if I do my duty by my folk. And know, as my father found out, the army of Wessex behind your back can be called out by the King at any time and dispersed. You know, your grandfather, Godwin, and the whole family were exiled with only their housecarls following."

"I know. I suppose you were in trouble then."

"Yes. We lost everything. Even Bosham was taken away."

"That sounds horrible."

"Your grandfather got us all back."

"Except for uncle Swein."

"Yes. Except for him."

"Did you ever fail, father?"

"Fail? Well…yes. I was once relieved of command of the King's ship. It was a bad day for me."

"What happened?"

"I rammed an enemy ship."

"Did you sink it?"

"No. I and my men leaped onto the boat and defeated its crew."

"So why were you relieved of command?"

"Edward was on my ship at the time, and he almost went overboard when we made contact with the enemy. He was so angry he told me I'd never command a ship again."

"But you command fleets."

"Yes. Things change."

"He seems to like uncle Tostig more than you."

"Yes. I think that's right."

"Aren't you afraid of dying father? Grandmother thinks you are reckless."

"I don't really…think about it. To die in battle is not such a bad thing, son. To die as a man, still strong, with sons to carry your name and brothers to bear your body."

"That sounds like old stories. I'm afraid of you dying."

"I do what is right for my kingdom and my folk."

"Do you like it?"

"War? I would be lying if I said I didn't son. There is nothing like the feeling of it. The raid on Rhuddlan. I only wish we had taken Gryffud, but no matter."

"Was it your plan to attack the Welsh capital?"

"Yes."

"And is it your plan when we attack the Welsh soon, father?"

"Yes."

"And the King agreed with everything you did?"

"Yes."

"So you are in charge, father."

"I serve at my King's will, young man," he grins at Magnus. "You see that church, there?"

"Yes, our church father."

"Our church? You know who owns that Church?"

"We do."

"It was a gift from King Edward to the Bishop." The boy's face changes to an expression of utmost seriousness.

"I understand, father."

"Of all my children, I know that you do." There is a tug on the line. "Let's see if we can catch something today."

*   *   *

Harold and Edith are settled against the bough of a tree, guards at a respectful distance.

"It has been some sixteen years since I met you."

"And your mother still hates me."

"I feel we have this conversation every time we are together."

"It never changes. Perhaps she can stay with Tostig in the North."

"If ever he stays there for long. It did occur to me. It would be good for Mor and Tostig both."

"Perhaps after the war, then."

"Yes, it will not be a long one. We burned a great part of their fleet at Rhuddlan, and the Irish are too good business partners to offer ships to Gryffud."

"It sounds like a fine plan, Harold. Less risky than the last one."

"Yes. Although the seasons are changing, and we may not have the winds with us."

"Will the boys be ready?"

"No, not at all. But they can march with Alfred and observe from a distance."

"Magnus wants to go," she smiles at the thought of him in mail.

"He will have to be given a role here. Perhaps the coastguard."

"He would like that. He loves fishing with you."

"Yes, a captain's mate on the coastguard, reporting in. It will be good for his letters. We'll have him learning trade too. Perhaps he can be on the Bosham-Southampton patrol. I'll have the reeve there take him through the ledgers. And he can learn his axe skills from the guard here."

"I'm staying here, Harold. At least until the war is over."

"That will be good for Gytha. She is kicking out against her skirts."

"What will the boys do Harold? When they are grown?"

"What I did, love, serve at the King's will. Support their father. Carve out a place. My brothers are earls and they have sons. Wyn will need more soon, too. Godwin will be Earl here. The others will be thegns."

"Perhaps we need to slow down."

"It may be too late for that my love," she nestles into him, this girl raised to an earldom by Harold's love.

"Harold?"

"Yes."

"Will Tostig manage in the North?"

"I don't know."

"I feel our family is always on the edge of success or destruction, both at the same time."

"After this war, our fortunes will be in our hands."

"Until the succession."

"Yes. There is also that, love."

*   *   *

Within six weeks some forty ships are assembled at Southampton, with twenty more promised at Bristol. With Harold's ten at Bosham there are seventy ships of men. Of his Housecarls, three hundred will be assigned to the ships, the Housecarls occupying fifteen ships with twenty sailors each. In the other ships will come Thegns and their men of the Fyrd with sea legs. Behind them ten more ships carrying supplies and spares. Once gathered, the ships and men are a plague on the town. Fights have already broken out, and the townspeople suffer under the burden of sailors and men freed from their wives. Harold himself is forced to ride out with Leofwyn and his men and police the town for two days. The site of mailed, mounted men, their axes and spears sharpened is enough to calm things and the Reeve is chastised for his lack of attention to order.

Walking together, back in Bosham Harold takes his old friend Alfred by the arm.

"The boys, Alfred. Blood them only if we have the advantage but use them someone. They cannot be left frustrated, or they will do something rash."

"Like you Harold," Harold smiles wryly.

"I fear that, somewhat, I do. But use them Alfred, so the men learn to work with them. I want them to be leaders, not sons."

"Yes Harold, I'll keep them in play."

*   *   *

Cartloads of salted pork, beef and fish are secured in barrels, along with pickled vegetables and fresh water and ale. The supply boats and longships are moored on jetties or beached and guarded day and night. After the tenth day of assembly, Harold calls the captains to him and gives their orders in his great hall at Bosham. Alfred and his group of warriors will accompany Ranulf, thegn and sundry others, along with members of Bishop Aelfgar's retinue, assemble in the fields outside Winchester along with the Fyrd of the counties of Wessex and half the king's own men, under Alfred's command until they meet up with Tostig. There, some fifteen hundred men march North to Tamworth to meet up with Gyrth. The boys have marched with them, mounted like the other housecarls, proud as their mother and grandmother wave them off. Young Magnus watches, itching to be with them and surly at the education ahead of him. Then Harold bids his wife goodbye, looking out at the sea. Wyn, too, holds his wife and baby in a bear hug and picks up his nursing son, looking the baby in the face.

"I have you to carry my name on now, Beorn. May you be like our cousin, noble, brave and good to your friends."

Godgifu, pretty and still plump stares at her husband balefully.

"When will it end, Win?"

"When it ends, love. We have a son now, and you have sisters, and he cousins."

"And land," says Harold throwing his arms around the pair. "Land and Welsh gold."

"A pretty pair."

"Like the both of you. Come now, lady, your husband will outlive his brothers, that I am sure of." He turns to the assembled captains.

"Men of the king's fleet! Assemble your crews. We sail for Wales."

There are cheers as Harold lifts his wife and youngest son and daughter all at once in a great hug. Then he turns with his hand axe at his belt and his fine tunic green against the brown deck of the Bosham pier. Time to sail again. This time in force.

The Welsh Campaign

Tostig and the men of the North tramp southwest to Tamworth, where Gyrth and the combined forces of Wessex, Mercia and East Anglia wait. He is almost a week late, but such things are expected, and the Northern showing is more than he had feared. Some fifteen hundred men from Wessex, a thousand from East Anglia and two thousand from Mercia added to his fifteen hundred make a fine army when half of the King's guard are added. Professional warriors, hardened men of the Fyrd, and the green shoots of unblooded men are coming together. They will operate in wings: Wessex and East Anglia in the middle and Mercia to the right. Tostig will take command position on the left with his men of the North and the King's housecarls. As they sit together, Tostig, Alfred, Gyrth, and Edwin, commanding the Mercian Fyrd on behalf of his father, brief the thegns assembled around them in their blue, green and brown tunics, gold at their necks and golden rings on their hands. Many have profited from Mercia's alliance with Gryffud, and this is an unwelcome campaign, though one they are loath to refuse. The Godwinsons are always waiting to snap up more of England and Harold's favourite brother is wanting for lands. Harold has sailed in advance of them, in order to meet up with forces at Portishead and strike out at Wales. They will march soon.

"It's been quite orderly, as far as these things go." In the last few weeks, Gyrth has busied himself in Mercia, organizing supplies with Edwin and instructing his own thegns to bring about some sort of cohesive training to the Fyrd armies of Southerly England. The forces are camped in orderly rows of undyed tents, interspersed by the odd noble tent died green or blue, beyond Tamworth, with as much expense as possible spent on keeping the men off the land.

Whores are in abundance under Gyrth's watch, a signal to the men to keep off the local girls. For the most part, save some scattered acts, the men are behaving.

"Given Mercia's…relationship with Wales we were very clear with the men that Edwin is not his father."

"And I appreciate that, I really do," Edwin says sardonically.

"Well Edwin, you let the fox in your henhouse God knows what the righteous farmer will do."

"I'm not sure that works as an analogy, Gyrth," Tostig says with a mild smile to break the tension between the two men. It's obvious Gyrth has been throwing his weight around. "I for one am happy we have a united England intent on a single foe. No Earls changing sides, no rebellion, no diplomacy needed; just a march westward in force."

At this the other nobles nod.

"You are changed, somewhat, brother," Gyrth acknowledges.

"This is much less complicated," he laughs with a humble nod of his head.

"The army is yours to command, brother, and we have young Godwin and Edmund with us."

"They are to be blooded, then. Soon it will be Skuli's turn."

"I feel my bones creaking at the thought of our sons turning into men."

"You are still young," Aethelgar nods to the men; his face is milder when he looks at Tostig now. Morcar sits happily by Tostig's side.

"So Morcar, you are to march with us?" Edwin strokes his drooping moustaches over a dimpled chin.

"With Tostig, brother, yes. It is fitting and I would be honoured to experience war at his side."

"I am surprised you have such faith in us Tostig."

"I do not know you for traitors. Besides, Harold will meet us at Ab-er-deffy—said it—and as we all know, a vengeful Harold is an army unto himself, let alone one with an army of seasoned men at his back."

"He is honourable, your brother. Our sister hates him of course, but he treated her nobly—you know he even had a man stationed to protect her in the heat of the raid."

"I know this. From that seed we can rebuild our amity, Edwin."

"Said like a true Christian, Tostig, let us move beyond past…old alliances and re-temper our nation in the furnace of Wales," Bishop Ealdred pats Tostig's arm and scans the room.

"I'll give my men two days to rest. Then we move. As soon as we reach the border, we must maintain cohesion. We cannot let ourselves wander into the Welsh hills."

"Yes brother."

"We need light scouts in front. Alfred, did Harold spare Wulfric?"

"No, lord, he needs him for the coastal campaign. But Wulfric will have his man meet us at the border. We will be hard to miss."

"And we trust this man?"

"He led us to Rhuddlan, lord."

"I'll tell you what we shouldn't do," Gyrth starts.

"And what is that?"

"What Ralph the timid did ten years back."

"Right, so nobody said we should all go on horseback, Gyrth."

"It's quicker if we have to flee, though."

"I don't think England can spare six thousand horses."

"What a sight that would be."

"Fuck off the pair of you," Earl Ralph, a large and red-faced man with a large scar down his face stands up and walks off. The other lords laugh heartily. Aside from the Earl of Mercia and Tostig's gang are Ansgar, Shire Reeve of Middlesex and Bondi the Staller, both loyal to Edward and unfriendly to Tostig and his brothers.

"Just us and the housecarls, then."

"Yes, we will flank the Welsh if we meet them in combat. Let's keep the scouts from going too far, I fear what those Welsh sing about in their poems."

"They can't just kill a man, can they? They have to gut him, piss in the hole, and fuck his skull before they consider him defeated. Then they write a song about it." There is awkward laughter.

"Let's do our best to avoid that then and recover our dead."

In two days, the army departs. Six thousand men, plus a thousand more baggage handlers, whores, priests and hangers on make as orderly a way as possible, monitored by Alfred and his hardened gang, who bring order with the butts of their spears and axes. First to Lichfield, where they are led in prayers by Leofwin and Ealdred combined; men kneel together and find the faith that only approaching conflict brings. Next, onto Stafford where the supply line is fixed. The army camps beyond the town borders with strict orders for anyone below the rank of thegn not to enter. The townsfolk are as scared of the Northerners as they are of Welsh reprisals, so their earl enters St Chad's with alms and dedications to the upkeep of the church there. Townspeople in their dun and tan peer at the tall Godwinson brothers next to their Midlands peers. The men who are not fighting either go about their lives or shift uncomfortably depending on their sense of Englishness. The less enterprising merchants scowl behind their stalls while those proactive ones make a beeline for the men around the earls; Copsig is swarmed with offers of wares and supply line support. All of this is encouraged by Gyrth, who takes control and forms a market of his own within the town square, taking bids on routes and goods in and out of the war zone.

"Bids on sheep, cattle and grain from Wales to Copsig. To Harnulf supply lines to the army."

"Thrall merchant here."

"No thralls."

"No thralls? Says who?"

"Says Archbishop Wulfstan."

"Oh him."

"Yes, and the King. Come see me after. I need more blacksmiths and wheelwrights. The king will pay for you, no need to bid. We need carts taking the goods in and bringing the injured back. We'll need men to go to St Chad's and men to Much Wenlock. And women, women to care for the sick – so make your wives and daughters useful. No, not in that way."

A second fyrd, the town defence, is called up. These men will patrol from here to Rodington, accompanying goods along the supply route – more as a deterrence against enterprising Welsh raiders than an effective fighting force.

On to the final staging point before their entry into Wales. Shrewsbury, at peace and safe from Welsh raids since the marriage alliance. Fear and suspicion everywhere here where the people are of a swarthier hue. The streets are emptier, houses burned and rebuilt in centuries of conflict silent in places where Welsh merchants and tradesmen and their families have fled to family across the Severn. Here, the army is assessed for a final time before the crossing. Housecarls from the four territories, along with archers and scouts hurry across the bridge to create an encampment lined with spears, in a half-moon shape large enough to hug an army. It is a wonder to these men that the Welsh have not burned the bridge yet. After a further day of contracts and victualing, the horde is off, leaving the river and ditches around Shrewsbury stinking with human waste.

"Armies leave their mark, even in friendly territories," remarks Morcar.

"We'll be fouling up Wales soon enough."

At the edge of the bridge Copsig finally cracks and begs leave of his Lord, who nods assent sourly.

The plain and painted shields of the four regions of England move slowly across the Severn bridge and in rowboats by the sides. England is marching.

* * *

Harold and his fleet reach Portishead on schedule. The weather has been threatening to break, and the ships have had to skirt the coast a little further out than in fair weather. One ship already has blown off course. It's a convenient place to beach ships without interrupting the flow of traffic and the course of the longboats rowing with the tide down to meet their comrades. Here they will load their special cargo and prepare for their initial foray into Welsh waters.

Assembling his captains, thegns, and warriors, Harold begins:

"Men, we will take Swansea and St Davids, dividing in two. Then we can raid the coast until we get to Conwy Bay. Leofwyn will raid down to Broad Haven while I secure Swansea after raiding up to that point. We raid, we burn, we leave. Then we meet and follow the valley until we meet with Tostig."

The men nod assent.

"If you are blown far off course, do not attempt to catch up. Your war is over. Go back to Bristol or Southampton. We are moving hard and fast and I don't want men butchered for no reason. We will manage. We will take our profit as we can. Move carefully through the towns and do not venture too close out. We want to herd these people towards each other, from two directions, not engage in full scale slaughter. Do not wander off and don't go it alone for a sneaky rape. They will get you and we cannot afford to waste time hunting for your butchered corpse."

"When Harold is this serious, you should all pay attention," Leofwyn grins at the men. There are chuckles, but the point is made.

"Once we reach Conwy we will reconvene, and the cargo can be unloaded. Then we stroke hard and reach Tostig and the land army. The fleet can depart. But captains – stick together. I think we burned the fleet, but you never know what deals these bastards can strike. Let's strike camp and eat fresh meat. We can depart in the morning if the weather is fair. And men, when we're done, there will be plenty of Welsh women wanting husbands, so keep discipline."

The next day the weather holds, and the ships head out under oar.

*   *   *

The young boys of St Davids are watching the fishing boats bobbing just off the Whitesands shore, the thin mists rolling like the waves, hazing their view. Their fathers, uncles and brothers are working while they idle, sometimes running off to play a game. One of the boys cries out as the high prows of longships appear on the horizon. They hear faint shouts as the fishermen realize their danger too late. Some boys run towards the shore while others scatter back to the town. Longboats crash through the waves upending the small boats unfortunate enough to get in the way. There is panic now. The thud of oars upon the waves and the great prows with their carved beasts are in sight now. And as if time accelerates the great sound of wood upon the shore as the ships beach and the fierce helmets appear. Helmeted giants glinting in the morning sun, armed with axes and spears, vault the sides of the ships and splash through the water onto the beach. Arrows skip through the air ahead of them as a great mass storms the beach and ploughs through the boys remaining. Beyond them the fishermen sit and drift helplessly. Here an order in a strange language is barked out and the large men form up. Men with bows come up from behind and the troop march at a fast pace towards the town.

Leofwyn and his band head up the white sands in as much order as possible. The shepherds flee at the sight of them, but they will not give chase. Wulfric has given a view of the town. This will be quick work. They march across open ground, pausing to set fire to the odd farm dwelling and hut. Those unfortunate enough to be in the way are cut down without mercy. The air begins to smell acrid as they head down the valley to the holy town. After some time, the small Cathedral appears ahead of them, and they spy what pathetic force the town can muster. The men drop their weapons and raise their hands. They are about to be corralled when an arrow thuds into the shield of one of the English warriors. All hell breaks loose. English archers release volleys towards the town and the men form up, shields raised higher. The town garrison is cut down and the men begin to charge through the mud streets.

"Spare the priests, women and children," their lord shouts. Any man left not out to sea is killed and a man caught climbing down the side of a hut is tackled and beaten to death. His bow rolls down the thatch as he gives his last grunt. Then they light the place up. Every building save the Cathedral is burned. The Bishop, Joseph, is out with his priests and monks, and watches the scene in dismay. With any small threat neutralized, Leofwyn, splattered with blood, lifts his helmet.

"Quae cosa est causa istae ruinae?" The thin Bishop looks at the young man in disbelief.

"Rex tuus est causa. Men, let's move."

They march back to the beach, past bodies old and young; those too slow to get out of the way. One boy lies curled on top of a younger one, his arms wrapped protectively. Leofwyn moves to shake the boy, but he is still. They move on, back the way they came, leaving the treasures of the Church untouched. Harold's way. Or perhaps Edward's.

Up to Cardigan, burned and rebuilt numerous times after Irish and Norse raids, where they beach in the early morning light. Same as before they line archers on the ships as the warriors haul themselves over the sides. They trudge over the dunes up towards the hasty palisades of the village, herons startled into flight, and the people just stirring. They pause at the gate while a few warriors haul themselves up the Norse way, using axes slung over the palisades, and over. There are shouts of alarm, but the gate is unbarred without fuss and they proceed through the encampment, methodically rounding the people up like sheep. They herd them out of the gate and force them into the fields beyond. Young boys and girls trapped in terror where they stand, their woollen clothes damp, will be made into servants for the men, their bereft parents left beyond, forced out to call for help. And that help if it comes with fuel the fires of panic.

Here the crews will rest in unburned huts. Some stray villagers are set to work bringing wood and kindling for a great bonfire on the beach.

The next morning, Asgar, on the watch, shouts the alarm. The men are ready. Some three hundred mounted Welsh warriors approach the village, just out of arrow reach. They've been tracking the English it seems. Following the path of destruction. Waiting for a chance to catch them napping.

"Our rides, lads," Leofwyn smiles. The men chuckle. Taking their shields and pulling rough helmets over their heads the men file out of the east gate and form a line, taking a slightly sidewards gate with left feet forward. Behind them, archers and a rear guard. The horsemen shift forward as one, causing the line of English to move.

"Steady, steady, keep the shields tight."

The horses shift again, these warriors in their boiled leather tunics, or occasionally mail, dull in comparison to the uniform bright steel mail of the English Housecarls. They paw forward again, and the nod is given to unleash a round of arrows. With a single low whistle they fly, landing just shy of the lead horses. With that, the horsemen wheel and head off at a gallop past the palisade and down towards the beach. A lucky arrow takes one down, but the rest charge past towards the ships.

"Round, men, round," march quickly.

The Welsh gain sight of the boats, too late they see another group form up. As they slow, the morning light rising behind them, volley after volley aimed at the riders fly. Men fall and the stocky ponies scream. The quick thinking among the riders turn again and head back West, wheeling and panicking at the sight of more men falling upon them. Some seventy fall, and the rest head off to spread the word. Four hundred English soldiers landed. Who knows how many more. They spend the day clearing the dead and burying them out of the reach of their noses and collecting what horses they can.

In a day they will light the fire.

* * *

As Leofwyn sails to begin his raids, Harold makes for the small fort of Newport. Word has been sent from Bristol to all the border towns to be on watch for counter raids, but the hope is that the Welsh will have garrisoned their ports and border towns after the initial raid, reducing the threat. Positioning ships loaded with archers at the estuary, they beach at Newport sands, just across from Portishead. It is a good first landing and the assemble in order before hauling two rams off the ships and proceeding up the grassy flats to the hill fort. The sky is heavy with passing rainclouds as the mailed warriors clunk in loose formation with their shields raised at an angle against arrows. And the arrows come like spatters of rain against a deck. The men duck down behind their shields. Hardly a threat, the arrows fall harmlessly in front. Harold gives the word and a group head towards the gate, gripping the iron handles of their rude ram. Men holding shields above them track their stumbling march as the hundred English archers start loosing arrows against the men on the six or so watchtowers ahead of them. The first thud against the gap between the two halves of the gate. Then the next. Archers above try to get a good angle, their hair a mixture of blond and black and red, products of waves of settlement and violence on these shores. All are Welsh now, just as the swarthy Wulfric knows no other folk. Asbjorn is held back as his brother heaves the ram. No need for both to risk their necks. Finally, the gate creaks and sags as thuds are heard in the distance – the second crew has made it round to the North gate, where they repeat the breaching attempts. Ladders go up against the towers now the guards hang lifeless from their posts and lightly armoured archers begin to climb, hanging on before the top as they wait for the rams to breach. And at the breach, they climb into position.

The South gate breaches, and big Olaf hauls his body against one side of the door to clear it. Then the ram is thrown aside to a short volley of arrows. They scramble to the sides of the gate as the volley slams into the shield wall prepared behind the wrecking crew. The men of the wall move forward, absorbing arrows, while their archers begin the careful picking of targets. Ahead of them a Welsh gang behind their own wall holds firm. The English wall enters the breach and the wrecking crew back off, leaving the larger housecarls following up in the rear armed with spears and axes. The wall fans out a little, keeping tight formation, adding men to the wings slowly as they enter the fort. Harold himself is right behind them, calling encouragement, urging them to tighten their shields as they move, left feet forward and long Norman shields tight together.

"Hard in boys."

The shield wall moves quickly and slams against the Welsh wall. They push as the big men Cyneweard, Harold, Olaf and Harald the Dane stab spears and swing their axes from behind the leading group. Arrows whip in from above, into the helmets and bare heads of the defenders. Shields and necks are hooked, the crunch of bone and spurts of blood becoming drowned out by screams. Two men of the Welsh group go down in front. They are packed tight. Now there is space and Harold roughly shoves through from behind his own wall and charges into the Welsh line. He is through the two-man deep wall he turns and swings his axe in an arc slicing two men from behind.

"Coming through Harold!" Olaf gives his warning and Harold shifts to let the big man through. They begin to swing and sweep their axes, now high now low until legs are separated from trunks and the screams fill the air. The wall collapses and the English keep tight, letting the big men through a single gap as they finish the job. Onwards now, through the irregular tracks between the huts onto the small longhouse and beyond as the North gate breaches. They break ranks and charge the rear of the smaller Welsh wall here just as their men come through the gate. They barely have time to finish their work before they collide with their own. All around, the sound of screams, of women cursing. The place is secured within a short time and the headman tracked down attempting to flee. They take what poor gold there is and set fire to the hall.

"Shall we burn the place lord?" Ragnald has his torch at hand.

"There is much blood here," Wulfric cautions his chief. Harold nods.

"We'll go easy on them. Send the headman out alone. These people have kin in England by the looks of them. No need to make an example."

One man dead, an archer called Oswald. For the rest, nicks and scratches, as expected. No major harm from this small fort. It's a good sign.

"We'll bury this man at sea," says Harold. He'll be dug up and humiliated otherwise. The day is spent making stakes and fortifying. They burn half the fishing boats down by the shore and hold the townspeople outside the palisades of Newport while they settle down for the night, feasting on fish and ale from the village stores.

They break camp the next morning the shivering villagers huddled together and helpless under guard.

"Let's fire up the North walls and leave."

The men of the final watch heave off their armour and settle into rest, back-to-back and shoulder-to-shoulder on their longboats as the sailors heave off. They communicate with horns and flags hoisted up on the masts and travel in a narrow arc. The transport ships will follow on to Cardigan under an escort after four days lag, hoisting sails across the channel and making as much time as possible. Haste will be imperative as Harold raids up the coast with Leofwyn making land further up. There they will divide the Welsh coastal watch, who expect the English to strike as one group.

On to Cardiff where they attack the hall of Gwrgan ap Meurig at night. Much like Bosham, the place is defended by a simple palisade and they make short work of the guards. This time, the lord is caught and brought to Harold. Wulfric, delighting in the capture of this man for unspoken reasons, translates.

"The Lord (he says the term mockingly) Gwrgan is asking what the cause of this raid is, after so much destruction at Rhuddlan." Gwrgan is a wiry man, who unfortunately for him came to collect the springtime rents. He sits unhappily on a bench in front of Harold.

"If he needs to ask then he forgets the actions of his king and people, and most likely, himself, on English trade. Raids on English border towns, capture and enslavement of English folk."

The Welsh lord shrugs, these things are commonplace.

"No matter why, we are here. Ask him how many men he has."

"He won't answer you, Lord."

"Then I'll tell you what. Let's keep this Gwrgan under guard on one of our ships and break my rule. We'll head inland and burn some houses until we can smoke these soldiers out."

"As you say, lord. Where do we keep Gwrgan, then?"

"Let's put him on a ship and keep him at sea until I return."

That day, Harold and half his men head inland, past farmsteads and hamlets. They fire up every other house and kill any man foolish enough to run out with a spear or axe, but no band of warriors materializes. The people stand around helpless in the face of such destruction, the Viking raids have long since passed into memory and folk song here, thanks in no small part to the English coastguard. Now they are a part of those sad songs themselves, and weep like those unused to war. The English head back to the hall and clean their armour and spears, resting for the night while the miserable Gwrgan sits lonely in a ship, surrounded by English sailors threatening always to throw him in the sea. The next morning Edgar, thegn, approaches his Earl, and places a companiable hand on his back. Harold looks up at him and smiles.

"Where next, lord?"

I say we take Gwrgan and go to his capital…"

"Lantwit Major, lord."

"Lantwith Major. And let's see if we can have a bloodless victory and disarm his gang. No need to burn the whole damn coastline if we can strike a deal and take some revenue for Wessex. The goal is to draw Gryffud out. We'll take their gold, too."

"I'll gladly take that, Earl Harold."

"Raping and killing the women will just harden the men's hearts. Killing their children will make them feral. I want to take their gold and burn their lords' halls, so they're sore at their king and willing to talk. I'd like a good stand-up fight too."

"I'll take that too."

"Wulfric? How popular is Gwrgan?"

"Well liked enough lord."

"So, his men will their spears for him?"

"I think so, lord. Stroke of luck capturing the poor bastard."

"I suppose we'll have to see. Let's start to treat him like the lord he is. Bring him back and let's feed the man and have him groomed and dressed."

It is fifteen miles to Lantwith Major. They will march there and have the ships follow under oar. Enough horses are found for the thegns, Harold and the Welsh lord, whose mount is tied to Harold's. Two mounted archers are placed behind him, and they are ringed with warriors. Despite his capture, Gwrgan is in fine spirits. Avoiding devastation is the best result under the circumstances and Gryffud has only slight influence here. The chance of resuming trade with Wessex after almost fifteen years of embargoes and maintaining Mercian trade is a topic of conversation as they ride to their destination.

Wulfric plays the translator again, his mother's tongue pressed into him from birth.

"Ask him, Wulfric, why the Welsh torture their defeated enemies to death."

"You could ask me to, Lord, but very well, one moment.

He says it's tradition."

"Tradition."

"If I were to hazard a guess – humiliating a man destroys the memory of him. This great warrior screaming and pleading to die while they slice him open and spill his guts—"

"And cut his cock off."

"That too."

"It destroys his living memory. All the time I've spent at court and in diplomacy with these people: I've always wondered but never asked."

"I don't think anyone really knows, to be honest. We just do what our fathers did."

Gwrgan grins at Harold and shrugs.

"We're a funny lot, but you know what's funnier? The further West in England you go the darker the lot of you are. But you still call yourselves English. I think you're all more like us than you like to admit."

"So, you speak English."

"I didn't want to upset your man here. He seems to need a purpose in life." Wulfric scowls.

"You hear that Wulfric – you thought you were finally useful and now you're being played for a fool." Hereward laughs and kicks his horse forward to scout ahead.

"And I think it is as he says, Earl Harold, or is it Jarl? It turns the hero into a squealing rabbit torn apart by a fox. And the fox can strut back to his people made greater still."

"I've killed many men, lord, and I can't say I take pleasure in their pain. Satisfaction from their deaths and my survival certainly. Pride at besting a fierce opponent. But causing pain for the sake of it? That does remind me of the suffering caused to Christ." Harold shakes his head. "It seems like a tradition that goes back before our God came to these isles."

"Earl Harold, did you have an epiphany on the road to Gwynned?" The men laugh at Oswald's quip.

"I pray like the rest of them. I just don't need a damned priest at my side taking my coin every fucking day." The men laugh heartily; even Gwrgan laughs along with them.

"So how would you like to proceed, Earl Harold."

"We will ride up to your fort and talk with your men."

And so they do. Wulfric and Harold's bannerman ride up to the fort; the pennant of Wessex waving in the breeze. The fort is larger than Cardiff with men at the watchtowers primed to fire at them. The palisades stand twice the height of a man and all the English can see is the smoke of homesteads. This place would be a challenge to take, but they would take it nonetheless. Harold watches his prized man off in the distance nervously. Watching his own archers to make sure their nerves don't get the better of them. After a series of exchanges, the gates are opened, and four men ride out. Two look like Gwrgan, sons, dressed in fine tunics, with gold adorning their necks and arms.

They raise their hands. The debate begins. Gwrgan and the four men start slowly, each taking their turn, before one of them spits and raises his voice in the complex canter of the Welsh tongue. Gwrgan shouts him down but he turns his horse and raises his fist. Some twenty men ride out of the gate and take off with him into the fields beyond. Harold stays his men. The other three nod to their lord and hand their weapons over to some of the English warriors stationed around them.

"So, lord Gwrgan, who was that?"

"My youngest. He'll go to the High King now."

"So be it. I want your men to stack their weapons outside the gate for now. We'll remain here. I'll be taking you or your son with me, so make a decision tonight. Your women are safe. Not sure about the pretty thralls."

Gwrgan gives his orders to his son and men and they ride back to the fortress.

"You are my guests I suppose."

"I think for tonight you are ours," laughs Harold. We'll be keeping a close watch, believe me.

That night they feast while the English swap places with the Welsh at the gates, which are barred tight. Bonfires are placed many paces beyond the walls and the men take short shifts to remain vigilant. Harold and Gwrgan talk long into the night with their thegns about old scraps and legends.

"Truly I though Gryffud was a new Arthur. But perhaps he is a Vortigern." Gwrgan shakes his head rubbing his dark beard speckled with white.

"I have heard of these men. Old kings when the Saxons first came to these shores."

"Vortigern brought you and Arthur fought you, and yet here you are," the Welsh lord smiles.

"And here you still are."

* * *

The next day they take to their ships with Gwrgan's eldest, also called Gwrgan, as their captive. Harold has taken the time to write a note on parchment taken from a priest detailing the trade agreement between the people of Gwynned. He makes two copies in his own hand and signs it with a special sign known to his reeves. His men watch with a mix of admiration and bemusement: this great warrior carefully detailing out the minutia of trade between two folk in the midst of a raiding campaign.

"Oh yes, lads, I'm quite the Hebrew. But this is how I pay you all so handsomely without needing to spill your blood and the blood of others needlessly."

"You are a wonder, Earl Harold," Olaf says admiringly, "perhaps you could write of your own deeds one day."

"Now there's a thought, Olaf."

With Glamorgan pacified after barely a fight, they move on. Across the shores of Deheubarth to the Gwendraeth estuary. They beach on the sands in the late morning, taking time to eat. According to Wulfric and Gwrgan, the estuary itself is too perilous to sail a fleet up. The chances of getting caught up on a bad tide and stuck in the mudflats made timing imperative. Far easier to march and maintain a safe position for their ships while they take Kidwelly. Four ships under oar filled with bow-armed sailors and dedicated archers will move to the Kidwelly shore while the four hundred English warriors march up the beach. Moving fast, Wulfric and a handful of men race up to capture a few strays as Gwrgan the younger watches on under a friendly guard. These men in their patchy yellow and madder tunics and breeches submit quickly and are prodded into revealing the best paths through the bogs. Here the English march, their feet clinging to the wet mud as they trek through the marshlands; they march in the moist air, clouds hanging low over the Welsh soil until they reach the low hills around the settlement. Here they take stock of the enclosure. An earthwork mound rises up some ten feet at a slope too gradual to be much threat from the North. The usual palisades rise up and in the village cries of alarm go up as the men assemble what small force they have.

They take the small fort without much of a fight and set the people on a course to the beach. There they march up to Carmarthen. The land is a mixture of pasture and rough grazing with oak ash and hazel copses along the valley slopes. They have no horses this day so a vanguard is sent out with Wulfric to scout ahead. Word must have reached the town of Leofwyn's raiding as the gates are shut tight. Men with ladders are moving along with as many torches as can be carried. The fort is surrounded by verdant farmland and rolling hills, and when the sun peeks through the clouds the men stop to gaze before their butcher's work begins. The fort is built on a hill with ancient stone walls repaired by rough timber. The approach is uphill though not overly steep. They will need to rain fire on the guardposts to limit their own casualties.

Thegn Edgar approaches Harold with Ulf, another thegn from Wessex.

"Harold, perhaps we could lead the assault today? You're risking yourself a lot on these raids." Harold shrugs and nods assent.

"If you will lads, but go hard and fast and mind you guard the men at the rams.

So Edgar and Ulf take the great ram with them and head at a fast pace towards the North wall. Harold gives the signal to his flag bearer who waves the Dragon towards the archers. Harold and his rearguard watch as the mailed figures move slowly up the rise towards the gate. Time passes and Harold is growing restless. A English carl falls and Harold strains to see who it is. The man sits up like the undead and pulls his shield back over his arm but he is struck by an arrow in his mailed chest and goes down again. Two of his brothers pull him back from the fight. Torches lit, warriors begin to fling fire at the towers around the gatehouse and the methodical beat of the ram against the gate begins. Another man goes down. The screams of women and children begin in pockets. Harold takes the remainder of his men and rushes towards the east wall, ladders in their hands. They prop them up against the stone walls, arrows shooting overhead and thudding into wood and men. The Welsh have focused their attention on the gate and the English under their Earl climb the four ladders and rush into the town just as the gate shatters. Archers stand on top of the walls and in the towers and the English rush the town.

"Keep it steady men!" Edgar and his crew form a shield wall and move through the fort in a tight group as Harold and his men run into the backs of the defending Welsh. Here the screams and curses ring out as the Welsh line breaks and the English spread out through the town, cutting down men and firing the place up. There is a monastery here, that they area at pains to avoid, although a few monks join the fray and are beaten down with the buts of axes and spears where possible. Some over eager warriors cut them down without mercy but there is no general slaughter. Harold eventually calms the place and makes peace with the abbot. They will use the fort as a base to raid in a ten-mile sweep, pushing the people into the midlands of Wales. The abbot, stern and devout lectures Harold on killing other Christians while they sit at dinner. In turn the Earl relays Edward's admonition to tread lightly on Welsh backs.

That night the screams of men wake the gang from their rest. Harold orders the men to stay within the fort. Once the screams subside, he settles back to sleep in the priory, itself a hotchpotch of stone and timber. The next day they move out in two bands, and find two of their men butchered and their guts laid open for the crows. He will not stay his hand here despite the dead men disobeying orders and the region is lit up without quarter. They will only move in daylight in this unfamiliar land. Wulfric is a constant presence, directing Harold's attention to ambush spots and dens. By mid-afternoon the smoke from the bonfires of villages will be seen for miles around. Six dead total, including the two fools who ventured out. Leif, who raided Rhuddlan, with his lord for eight years, has fallen, dead just beyond the gate. The area has suffered for it. As they leave they light up Kidwelly for good measure and take all the food they can.

They move up the coast, firing up the small and large villages, venturing only as far as a daytime march will take them. They return to discipline, not wanton destruction. At Milford Haven there is an ambush as they head from their ships. Riders on stout ponies hammering into the great men. The English are quick to react and their archers who have hung back with the rearguard run quickly up and begin their work. Here the size of the housecarls counts in their favour and they give each other space to haul their axes around. The initial charge downslope is tempered by the sheer size of the armed men and the Welsh cavalry struggle to disengage as the rearguard rushes up and to the side. Harold himself is in the thick of it, looping his Dane axe at the legs and feet of the horses, his fine armour darkening with blood and the screams of the Welsh battle cries and death throes. There are English dead too, here, and the thrashing horses start to threaten even more lives. Harold barks and order to back off and they disengage and form a wall of shields in an arc. Ivar falls, slipping as he tries to back into formation, others too, struggling under the weight of dead horses and men are trampled on. The archers loose their arrows more freely now and the attack slows.

"Cease firing!" Harold bellows and charges out from the protection of the shields, his own shield thrown on the ground, hammering at the horsemen, blood gushing from arteries as he carves man and beast. There the English break ranks again and begin their work. So few of the Welsh horsemen have fine armour that the fight becomes a slaughter and the few who can turn their horses and head down the valley. Six here. six good men and others injured too. They start to haul the horses off their dead to find Ivar's fine helmet crushed beneath the weight of horses' hooves. Those horses still thrashing and the Welsh in their death throes are ended quickly and the dead separated. They do as they did to the region around Carmarthen in honour of their dead, their lord at the head of them like a burnished demon, sparing only those their King has demanded. The lands here are full of farms and livestock and they have villagers herd the animals down to the shore where they spit the animals and feast to their comrades' memory, making the miserable peasants serve them. Young Gwrgan watches impassively: these must not be his folk. At dinner that night, a woman brought to serve the men takes a dagger from the folds of her skirts and stabs a sailor in the neck with a knife repeatedly until two men shake themselves out of their shock and take her down. They end her in front of her folk and drag her body into the sea. It is all Harold can do to stop another slaughter.

"Lord," cautions Wulfric.

"I know, we have been too careless since Gwrgan. Is Cardigan near?"

"Not far, lord. Your brother should have things ready for us by the time we reach it."

"Straight sailing from here. We've done enough damage and I'm sure Wyn's been busy."

They organize the dead and wounded onto a ship and send it back down towards Bristol in the hopes that men may be saved and the dead buried on friendly shores before they bloat and reek.

"That's a ghoulish one, that longboat," Thegn Ulf shakes his head.

"A ship of the dead lord," nods Hereward, nursing a bruised shoulder.

"Our plan can't come soon enough," Harold muses. He is stripped to a tunic while men scrape gore from the hauberks before putting each into a barrel full of sand and rolling it around. Pissing on Harold's armour is forbidden, but vats of vinegar are brought to burnish it to a fine sheen before they set off again. This time, women are taken to serve the men, after the death of the sailor and the ambush. It only takes a few deaths for the old ways to return and the king's reach shorten. They set off as the sun's own reach diminishes and safely offshore, they sail under the evening light towards Cardigan.

It is another day before they see the great cloud of smoke billowing up from the shore and the transport ships just ahead of them. They will beach at Poppit sands, the transport vessels, built by Flemish Shipbuilders beaching and the crew cajoling the great horses onto the beaches. They have lost a ship to a squall and panicked horses, and, as one crew unloads, another breaks free and knocks two men over, careening over the sands and off in a wide circle. Eight horses to a boat, they manage one hundred and twenty horses of the

European kind and sundry English horses of twelve to fourteen hands each. The disembarkation is painfully slow and Harold has his ships beach a little further down to avoid collisions. One by one the brown and black animals are goaded down the ramps and led in little circles to find their stumbling feet again. Down on their knees and pushed and pulled up they make their way up the sands to grassy pasture.

Leofwyn rides down to his brother on a Welsh pony, grinning as his long legs almost touch the ground. The two men embrace and exchange their stories, as the crews make sure the boats do not drift and drop their iron and wood anchors, dragging them into the sand as far as possible to stave of storm surges that could carry the boats off. Warriors and thegns give gentle thumps on his back as they pass him. The smoke on their journey over shows he has done well.

"Typical Harold: you intend destruction and end up making friends."

"We burned enough, believe me, and Milford Haven was a shock. I think a band on destriers would have done us in."

"It was a risk taking these horses, brother."

"They will come in useful, foot marches beyond the shore are risky. We still don't have clear knowledge of where Gryffud is. How many ponies did you manage?"

"About forty all told."

"We'll take them as pack animals. I think for longer trips we might ride the ponies and lead the destriers to keep them fresh."

"Let's not be too experimental brother. Ralph took a beating trying new things under trying circumstances." At the mention of

Earl Ralph there is much mockery and laughter from the men around."

"Ralph was outnumbered."

"You are kind brother."

They summon the thegns and captains to Cardigan and assemble in the hall.

"Wyn will take the bulk of the men and head up raiding until Aberdyfy. I'll take a hundred and raid inland. We'll fire the place up from coast to inland so the people move further inland and meet with Tostig's outcasts."

The sailors, many of them resourceful, improvise baths and sables from the wood they have. The ships are checked for leaks and damage from the horses. The men of the horse cargo ships are exhausted from their sleepless trip and the farriers with them are as hollow-eyed as if they have spent two months campaigning. Harold's men take their rest for a day or two and do their best to groom each other. Oswald is an excellent barber and is put to work on his lords, shaving their stubble and meticulously styling their fine moustaches. He whistles and hums contentedly as he works on his lords, nodding and murmuring platitudes as they talk of their worlds. The women they have captured are put to work boiling and scraping the tunics under strict guard. There is no outbreak of lice yet, although these women themselves have been forcibly washed and groomed much to their humiliation, to avoid any such outbreak. The men are under strict orders again. After the ambush, presumably by the same band that went after Leowfyn's gang, they wish as much as possible to keep a desperate enemy from their rear. The threat of punishment will be enough to make men think twice before raiding again.

Armor burnished, bellies fed, and horses settled under guard it is time to raid again. The transports will head home under a small guard of ships emptied of troops accompanied by what treasure the men have captured on their way. So the brother part again for a few days as they ravage the last few miles before they take Aberdyfy from two sides. Harold will begin quick and fierce raids up to Aberdyfy as the longships heave off, ready to burn the shore.

*　　*　　*

As the army assembles across the Welsh border two men on horseback approach. They are both dark skinned with the curly hair of the Welsh. The alarm sounds and the Army's leaders come to the front. Archers are at half draw as Tostig mounts his horse and, with his thegns about him rides up to meet the men.

"Are you Tostig?"

"Yes."

"Where is Alfred, then? I thought we'd get a warmer welcome." He has a broad face with a gat toothed grin and with him is a younger man, perhaps a son or brother. They are dressed in tunics of blue and green if a little worn, and their woollen cloaks have been carefully woven. Alfred is summoned.

"You look familiar, friend."

"He's Wulfric's cousin, Lord."

"We're kin, and close kin too."

"Close enough to betray your king for him."

"Gryffud claims kingship over all of us, but not all of us would have him as king."

"Your name?"

"Rhodri, and this is my brother, Hywel." Hywel nods at them. "He's not much of a talker. Best be off then, Earl, all of Wales knows you're coming. Before we go, I do have a favour to ask of you."

"Ask."

"There's a certain area I'd like you to spare if you would."

"Yours, I presume?"

"Where my family are, yes."

"Show us and we'll leave it be. It might have been best if you'd brought them with you."

"Well, that's the thing…"

With that, the great army moves, the bridge over the Severn with its Fyrd guard slowly left behind at the beginning of the English supply chain. Men march with their shields and weapons, although most of the housecarls are mounted. Harold's sons ride up front with their uncles, eagerly asking questions and taking in the lush green fields around them. They will cut South rapidly, assuming the Welsh army will expect an immediate march West or North. Here they find the first of the Welsh settlements and pass through with little resistance, burning houses and setting the fields smouldering. For now, the men are disciplined and their watchful shepherds ride around them, keeping the killings light. Bishop Ealdred, armed with a mace, blesses the men as they begin their methodical destruction, laughing and joking as they casually herd the villagers into cattle pens and taunt them as their homes burn. Spread out two miles wide with horsemen ravaging five or so further out, they cut a band of destruction, following Rhodri's direction. Village after village they come to until there are no villagers, just empty houses as they flee

West or South towards others fleeing from the coast. Such misery they visit upon the land, they'll wreck the harvest here and force the wretches to trade for every loaf of bread with England. At one village an old woman hobbles up in her rags and waves her stick at Gyrth, cursing in her native tongue.

"A witch," one of the men cries. Gyrth clutches his throat and chokes. For a second there is stunned silence before he bellows out a laugh.

"Perhaps. Fetch a priest and have her performed on; she is either mad or possessed."

They fetch a callow priest in his twenties, short and slightly built. He trundles up to the old woman and holds her by the shoulder, pressing his cross against her forehead. She spits on him and hits him with her walking stick. Then she starts to beat him until his faith breaks and he flees her. There is laughter from the men. Gyrth dismounts.

"Begone, foul witch and never blight this land again," he intones.

"I think it's us blighting her land, Earl Gyrth," his housecarl, Ethelgard laughs.

"You make your point fairly." The old woman begins to beat the great man in his mail coat. He lets her wear herself out before he takes the stick from her and sits her down.

"Check her for a knife, lord!"

"Hang her for the Welsh witch she is."

"She's just an old crone. Leave her some food and find me someone who talks her language. We'll leave her hut be and bring her some food you men. She reminds me of the Richeldis woman." They all laugh, except for the priests and a few devout men who shake their heads at the Earl. "Perhaps she can build us a hut for the holy mother here."

They find a translator and have the woman name her hut. Then they light the huts away from her and leave her muttering alone.

"If the Welsh fight as hard as that we'll be in for a rough ride, lads."

They are marching in units as they would assemble in battle. Gyrth on the right with horsemen flanking him and burning. Tostig in command position on the left and, sandwiched between the brothers, Edwin, Ralph, and Ansgar, whose distrust of the Godwinsons runs deep. It is obvious that he is Edward's agent, so they keep him with the men of Mercia. He can report on their actions.

On the fourth day the flanking scouts are late coming back and Gyrth sends a man to Tostig to halt. Gyrth's two thousand wheel to face the West and form up, waiting for the rest of the army. Ordered to disengage, the absence is worrisome, so Gyrth has his men start West in a line until they reach a town, more substantial than the assemblage of huts they have found so far. He kicks his horse on to view the devastation – signs of resistance here, men with weapons dead, women too, some still living, their skirts torn. Fearing an ambush, he has the men form into two wings and skirts the town, moving past the dead. There is smoke up ahead, too. He calls his mounted warriors to him and has the fyrd maintain their line before riding off towards the rising cloud. There the scouts are busy burning and fighting with what resistance the locals can put up. Gyrth and his men kick their destriers and ride into the midst of the melee. The scouts have dismounted and fighting hard with some fifty Welsh warriors, the dead piling up. They ride around the outskirts of this village and dismount before moving around some thatched house as a group. Some hundred East Anglian warriors raise their shields and begin a charge into the Welsh flanks. There is cursing and screaming in two languages as the highly trained infantry of England squeeze the Welsh from two sides until they crumble and fall in a heap of dead and dying. They take two prisoners from the dead and strip them of their leather jerkins, sending them back for questioning. Only a third of the scouts are here, some forty men and sundry dead two.

"What happened here," Gyrth snaps at one of the men.

"They surprised us, Earl Gyrth, while we were pulling the huts down."

"You mean pulling your breeches down, you dumb dogs."

"No, lord."

"I saw it back at the other town. Where are the rest?"

"They carried on lord, to chase some horsemen."

"So they fooled you."

"I suppose so lord."

"You suppose so. Take three men and get on after them and bring them back."

"I'm not sure where they went to exactly, Earl Gyrth, we were busy here."

"I'll find them lord," one of Gyrth's housecarls says. "Just need to follow the hoof prints."

The others are found and returned within a few hours. Their horses are tired and they lost six more men. The dead are collected and transported by cart to Shrewsbury. It is not a good start.

Tostig eventually catches up to them.

"We've lost discipline already. Bring the men here." He chastises them for their foolishness in front of the army assembled up in front of them and has Gyrth do the same. Godwin and Edmund sit atop their horses watching it all.

"Will they be punished more?"

"We'll pay them a bit less at the end. No need to start a riot so soon."

The army camps for the night, ditches and latrines dug and a watch set comprised of the right-wing cavalry, miserable and tired after a day of gleeful destruction.

Having lost a day, they slowly turn back in the South-westerly arc and head down. A rearguard headed by Morcar and Ansgar is formed up.

"No better way to keep a man loyal than to have him take the brunt of an attack on our rear," Gyrth tells the boys. They nod sagely but wonder to each other why you would trust a snake at your back.

"Because the snake is watching his tail the whole time," their uncle overhears them, they remain unconvinced. "And Ansgar is with them. He may hate our family but he is loyal to Edward so he'll keep Morcar from trouble."

Edwin is being watched too, and he knows it. The fate of Mercian leadership depends on this campaign and both Ralph and Leofwyn are waiting for one wrong move to take their place. The army tracks across the open terrain of Llandrindod Wells where there are scant pickings. A few men desert east in the direction of Kington, taking their chances before they get deep into Welsh territory. Alfred and a core group of the King's own guard are sent off after them; they round the terrified men up and strip them of their weapons, shields and helmets, all supplied by the king. Then they take them back and get their names from their fellow soldiers under threat of fines and loss of hides. So named and inscribed on parchment by their local thegns, they are released off into the wild. Men of no honour, to be tried and fined or stripped of land if they make the return journey home. And if some Welsh band catch them, so be it. Their pleas to be allowed to return are met with deaf ears and they are turned from the army as pitiful as the peasants they have taken from their homes.

"Harsh for a first offence, brother," Gyrth would have preferred to make a mockery of the men and have them dig the latrines, but Tostig is alert to the previous day's scouting disorder.

"They need to understand it's us or the Welsh. We need to maintain discipline before we become a mob and the Welsh begin to pick at our bloated mass like crows."

"Very poetic."

"We are being tracked for certain," says Rhodri, "those boys won't last long now."

"You visited death on those men."

"And the rest will know it," Tostig is becoming harder the further they march, his eyes bright and his body released of its burden; men shift from his gaze and make way without the slightest delay.

The Welsh Campaign

"You are back, Tostig, or coming back. I hope we meet with battle before you scare the men to flight."

"Fear not, brother, we need a clean campaign, and the king has his eyes everywhere among us; our favour can shift with the winds here."

"I dread the thought of Edward coming to 'bring order'. We'll be marching South one day and North the next. We'll be like a dog chasing its tail by the end of a week, going on a hunt every third day, forgetting why we came here and marching back the way we came to plan the campaign all over. Then we'll make a new treaty and celebrate our great victory with two weeks of prayers."

"So, let's keep order ourselves, then," Tostig lets himself smile at his brother. Then he starts to laugh, and the men around him, especially Athelgar, gape at this stranger among them.

Gyrth has provisioned Hay on Wye as a second supply centre. His nephews are surprised at this warrior uncle's diligence, until he gives them a stern lecture on the importance of trade, supply chains, logistics and learning. This most unpriestly of men proselytizes the Godwin way of the warrior trade with the same fervour as Harold's Goshawk lectures. Their father has equal fervour for knowledge and killing it seems, and they are encouraged to keep at their reading and sums. Even Tostig rolls his eyes and turns back to his scriptures. The rains have been light this spring and so they can cross the river at fording points, with only slight recourse to boats, although the carts have half their cargo removed as they cross. They see the distant figures of horsemen as they trek through farmland and small villages, the people having fled towards Brecon. Southwest under Rhodri's guidance they march and burn to the foothills of the Black Mountains where they camp with stakes provisioned around the camp and fires lit out beyond them. Servants make up tables and benches for the earls and thegns, who dine every night under canopies, while the men spit and roast their own food. Every night and morning there are prayers for the assembled army, becoming a running joke as men begin to ray as they piss in latrines and pray before they clean their weapons. Morale is high and the scouts are more obedient under Tostig's firm but not unduly harsh rule. His old reputation has returned and men know not to cross the man who brought the North to heel. Morcar is full of admiration for him, and Harold's boys grudgingly pay him respect, even before his first stand up fight, but they lean towards the earthy Gyrth with his ready laugh and ease among the men. A man more like their father, even if he is a mass of contradictions.

One night, Gyrth calls Rhodri to him and the other chiefs.

"Rhodri, what's your story then? A king ousted from his throne—and Wulfric the son of a Princess, your cousin?"

"We were mostly traders and large farm-holders to tell the truth."

"That is so disappointing. I always fancied Wulfric a vengeful prince of Wales."

"No, not at all; although we're all related to royalty here, there being so many fucking princes you can't move a few miles without bowing to some cunt."

At this the Lords laugh heartily.

"That's how England was once."

"And now you just have one cunt."

There is further laughter, muffled by Tostig's stern look.

The army moves through the Honddu valley, with scouts mounted on sturdy ponies surveying the land to the sides. There are skirmishes here and there, but the Welsh are not numerous enough to mount resistance and the English losses are few, and all injuries. Coming from the North over the Honddu prevents fewer obstacles including avoiding the river Usk, although most attention will be focused here. Tostig takes a day to survey the place, despite Gyrth's urges to storm. They will take their time here in their first real fight. Rhodri, gaining a reputation for omniscience, has given a detailed accounting of the Fort, or Ilys, at Brecon, and the two-to-three hundred men there. Villagers fleeing the initial march will have come to the fort, making life uncomfortable for its garrison. If they had the time they could starve the fort out and have them turn out their own people into the waiting English lines. It would be a chance to show the Welsh the mercy of the English and make future assaults easier. Perhaps they might even be handed over forts without a fight. But there is no time and after a day of scouting around the fort, Tostig chooses his positions and has the rams and ladders prepared. The Mercians are picked for the assault, with Gyrth and a select number of East Anglian housecarls joining. Tostig himself will stay with the main army so as not to risk three commanders in a low-risk fight, although he is chafing at the bit to see action again.

"Better you stay than Gyrth, Earl Tostig," Alfred says. "He'll lose his patience and charge in. You'll get your fight."

Earl Ralph, eager to lose his epithet, demands to be part of the fight and is not refused. Lacking sons, his property would be ripe for reallocation. A Godwinson back in Herefordshire would make amends for Swein's tenure.

"Just remember Ralph," Gyrth notes sagely, "horses can't climb walls."

Then the whole army prays willingly and eagerly for God to spare them this day.

They storm Brecon's wooden palisades with rams, ladders and the braying of horns. Ralph is first over when the ladders crash against the walls and hauls his large body over the slimy wood, swinging his axe at the Welsh defenders inside. Gyrth and his men follow, with the men of Mercia battering the gate on the North side. It is boggy, the rains having persisted, and the men in armour have a rough time of it, their feet clogged in the muck and the ladders wet from the morning dew becoming increasingly hard to climb. After much swearing and the occasional scream of a man struck by an arrow, the gates crash open and the general havoc begins. Such is the crush of people within, it is impossible for the men, if they had the inclination, to pick their targets with the weapons they have. A thousand English pouring into a fort made for three hundred men at most ends any thought of mercy. The Welsh do not lie down easily but they are pushed further back into the town with its hotchpotch of wattle and thatch houses and single stone and timber church. Eventually some inhabitants open the south gate and flee. The warriors, to their credit, stay within and move quickly between the houses, infuriating the English Fyrd, who are not trained to remain organized in this kind of brawl.

The screams of women and children begin as they hack furiously through the mass of bodies. With much difficulty they are brought back into order at the gates and formed into a wall by Edwin, as Gyrth and his housecarls press on under occasional fire. The men of East Anglia then proceed with their shields raised and spears and axes held at the half point. Some even discard their long weapons and draw their swords, hunting the mostly poorly armoured Welsh in packs through the bogs of the street. They fight with few casualties among the elite, although the Fyrd has suffered some, unarmoured as they are for the most part. And the core part of Tostig's strategy has worked. They come out blooded and thirsty for Welsh blood, these men for whom Welsh trade has been their making. Brothers, friends, and fathers lost. These men deposited with care on carts that rattle back under guard to Hay, with a promissory note written up by their priests and thegns to maintain their hide or holding and their family to receive pay double that of the man who returns to his family. For the most part, barring a few wealthy unfortunates, they will be buried at Hay or Shrewsbury and their personal effects stored and returned at the end of the war to what family they have.

Tostig rides into the town bathed in sunlight like a burnished statue in his helmet and polished mail. In the village square are strewn women, children and the elderly among the men who were cut down regardless of their bearing arms, eyes staring out at him from contorted faces, mothers cut through almost in half covering their children who lie as still as their defenders. Some half remain alive, and he has them put to work digging graves and latrines. There is no lord or under-king in the hall, which Tostig uses as his headquarters, stationing They station members of the fyrd here to keep the people from returning and rest the great army in the shadows of the Brecon mountains, so vast, even the Earls are awed by the green and tan ridges. They debate a detour to Castell Dinas, a fort and source of raids closer to the English border, but sounder heads prevail. So Tostig dispatches orders for the Fyrd of Hereford to station near the border and patrol for raids. On a still morning, the breeze clearing mists, armour cleaned and polished and the horses brushed to a sheen they fire the fort and leave Brecon for the grim passes of Tretower. There are riders on their stout ponies in the distance, tracking the army. The feint has obviously thrown Gryffud off-guard and the havoc the English army is causing will force him south. These riders are a good sign that they have been noticed and the brothers are eager for a fight. Harold or no. The army spreads out again through the Myddfai-Rhandirmwyn area, famous for its doctors. They light the land up, for the most part sparing the people so they flee Northwards, becoming a burden on their neighbours and sparking ancestral squabbles. Like a great swarm of locusts it empties the land wherever it travels but also leaves the filth of horses and men in its wake. A stampede, then, led by a man reignited.

To see him now, erect in his saddle and well-built, but with a lithe elegance about his large frame, his face that of a Dane softened around the cheekbones with his moustache thick and trimmed at the stern curl of his lip, were his eldest brother's crosses the face in a bar. His blue eyes are bright and his hair trimmed around his forehead. There is something that prevents him from being handsome, some strictness around the chin, a thinness perhaps where Harold's face is broader. Tostig meets men's eyes in a hard stare, where his brother's half gaze and lips always ready to smile giving him a charm that Tostig envies admiringly. On top of his blue gambeson, his fine mail, made by Danish smiths, and a gold chain with a large elegant cross with a central ruby around his neck. His sword hangs at his left side with his hand axe at the right, and his helmet, hung from his destrier's pommel, is richly decorated with a cross and wyverns around the brow. Gone is the slight bow of the head and the slumped shoulders. Men begin to look at him and gain confidence, where they seek comfort from Gyrth's jovial banter.

Edwin pales by comparison; his brown hair and average frame, common face, like a man dressed as an earl; but he is liked by his men, and is a keen arbiter of justice; fair, solid, dependable and wary of playing politics against the Godwinsons. His men, saltire painted on their shields, the golden cross of St Andrew on a blue background, go where he directs, and, now that they are blooded, look to him as their lord. He is close to Ansgar, whose pocked and scarred face seems a constant threat. Gyrth is told to keep his distance by his brother and let the man be Earl, after he was pushed aside in Gyrth's zeal to organize the army of the Midlands.

They harry the middle lands of Wales, until they reach Tregaron to the West of the brownish greens of the Cambrian mountains. Here

The Welsh Campaign

the roads become even poorer with rocks jutting out of the ground, and the carts need to run half empty, skipping up and down with animals carrying the burden. Their horses slow to a crawl on the uneven surfaces, almost like skittish deer. The ponies of the scouts make for better mounts, and they are drawn closer to the wings and circle about looking for the Welsh. Off in the distance to the west, they see the faint smoke of fires.

"Oddly comforting, that," Morcar notes as he rides to the left to meet with Tostig. Tostig nods agreement. Harold and Leofwyn's work.

It takes them three slow days to reach the environs of Aberdyfy. They camp with men patrolling all night, the odd their tents close together and the filth piling up around the land where they have camped. The rock is too hard to build latrines here. One night a man is killed, straying too far from the camp. His screams wake the six thousand men and cause a general alarm. But for the most part it is quiet. Gryffud seems to be forming his army to the North. The going is tough with wooded hills and the threat of ambush, as they trek towards their goal, some eighty riders come hammering in from the West. Tostig, on the left, forms his lines in as quick a format as he can, as the riders come in. The other leaders are quickly to push their horses on to meet with the threat.

"Ralph, you are redeemed," says Gyrth, as the banner of Wessex approaches them, whipping around in the wind.

"Perhaps the day has come," the Earl says, who has joined in with the jokes.

Harold pulls his horse up in front of the line of men.

"Not the best facing up," he bellows, and pulls his helmet off. Top to toe, dusty and his fine armour in need of a cleaning but he is beaming from the action. Tostig prepares himself, stiffening somewhat until Gyrth shoots him a look.

"Brothers, Lords…Ralph."

"Ralph the redeemed."

"You have the command brother," Tostig says in a strained voice.

"Yes, thank you." The brothers dismount and embrace, Harold careful not to pat his brother on the back. The boys rush out to meet their father and he looks at them sternly as they begin to hug. They stand up straight as manly as they can and then he grabs the pair of them in an embrace.

"Let's get our council together and share stories." A flat patch, away from any marshes, is found, where they can erect a tent, shelter from the coming rain. Barrels stand for chairs and minimal fuss is spent on the furnishings. A strong guard of a quarter of the army is posted around them and the Earls and thegns assemble around Harold.

All told, two hundred dead or injured; of them, mostly fyrd, but housecarls are the majority among the coastal raiders. They have burned some sixty villages, forts, and hamlets, and driven, not slaughtered, most of the population out.

"Brecon will be a point of contention with the King, but we had our times too," says Harold, rubbing at his stubble and fussing with his moustache, which is hanging over his lip. He is making eye contact today, at each of his brothers, the earls and thegns. Tostig sits at his right and Gyrth makes way for Edwin at the left, sitting down from Tostig.

"How did the horses fare," Athelgar asks.

"These big destriers are a nightmare to transport. In bad weather you have to contend with the storm urges and their skittishness. I'd say they're a safer bet for summer sailing. It would have been easier to have horsemen enter from the border but then then they would have been isolated at night in their camps. They are fine for raiding of course."

The Earls and thegns nod.

"There's not been much resistance, likely because Gryffud is converging his forces North. Bring Wulfric and Rhodri."

The two men enter the tent, both unfazed by the fine men around them.

"What's the news from the North?"

"Well since we've both been with your lot it's a bit hard to get exact information, but from what I gather, there's division between the King's counsellors, and a stand-up fight seems unlikely," Rhodri notes flatly.

"I wouldn't put it past Gryffud to risk a fight against us now we've stirred up the beehive," says Wulfric. "He needs something big after running away naked from his bed and leaving his wife at our mercy."

"Then again, he could make for the hills and make us run around in circles hunting for him," notes Gyrth.

"We'll take Aberdyfy with Wyn launching from the coast, and then take Machynlleth, as planned. Then we'll drive North together."

"The only thing to be cautious of," says Tostig, "Is our great mass of troops running into each other."

"Yes, that exactly. We'll mix the Fyrd and the Warriors up, not that our people aren't warriors, and post half the army as rear guard at Aberdyfy, then reverse that group at Machynlleth. We'll need to watch the rear and wings like hawks. Gryffud has always been one for the unexpected."

The next day they march on Aberdyfy. Riders have gone ahead to ensure Wyn is on time. He has already begun beaching the longships and the men of Wessex are beginning to form up and gather their gear. They take the Welsh boats and burn them, pushing them out to sea so as not to be smothered by the smoke or start a fire with their own navy. Some hundreds of boats, small and large are taken and the crews of any large war-boat killed. The rest are sent packing right into the middle of the English host. It takes a day, while the larger army converges and the Fyrd are sent to help in the careful destruction. It is as if the sea has caught fire for a while, then the smoke of some hundred houses across a bay. The villages scattered about the marshes are hunted through and anything that could be used as a weapon seized. Then as the ships bob out to sea and any threats are pushed off by long staves or oars, the longships form a blockade, cutting off any hope of escape for this region. Leofwyn now commandeers a horse and rides to meet his brothers.

The four Godwinsons gather in front of their men. Harold, blonde with that fine moustache running as a bar across his cheeks; large limbed and bearish though not overly so, feint scars across his face, and the sea biting him somewhat, though not enough to make him hoary. Gyrth, rounder faced and merry, his moustache as long as his brothers, hair cropped in the standard English cut and his body that of both warrior and a man fond of life; there Leofwyn, tall, leaner, and long haired in the Danish style, hanging down to his shoulders and his face angular, the eyes hooded and his eyes grey and mild today. And Tostig there with his brothers, one of them again,

The Welsh Campaign

the distance closed. The pack. Missing only their youngest brother, Wulfstan.

"Brother, you are reformed and burn anew," says Harold admiringly.

"I'm looking for a real fight," his brother says smiling more broadly than ever.

"I'm hoping Gryffud sees he has three choices—run, move North and draw us in or ambush us."

"The further he moves North, the more of a retreat it seems, and the greater the reminder of the Rhuddlan embarrassment there is."

"He's letting us get careless," says Edwin to the mass of Godwin. "He's like that at dice, and every other game."

"But we caught him out in the raid, and I don't believe he expected war," notes Harold.

"Nevertheless, he's quick witted and still has the bulk of the Welsh."

"Except for everything below us. He'll have a mass of farmers, fishermen and hangers on to deal with soon. Hardly the best situation for the army." Tostig is scratching at his own bear.

"We need two days' rest and baths. Let's get the people working and check them for knives."

The armour is scraped and rolled in barrels by soldiers and support, fresh tunics and breeches are brought out for the men, who go through the usual foolery of finding clothes that are the right size. There are plenty of men with baggy or tight breeches, switching and pranking and farting in the wrong pair until the whole situation is resolved. The lords are bathed, shaved and clipped and the housecarls and soldiers work on each other, finding streams and barrels to bathe in. Now some six thousand strong, they are formidable sight when dressed.

Harold, in command, will take command position on the left, with Tostig moving to the right.

"Demoted again," notes Gyrth.

"It's a double demotion," notes Tostig.

"I'm in charge," laughs Harold.

On the third day under a timid sun, the army assembles into three columns. There are riders on the wings and the baggage is secured by three hundred Fyrd. Marching to Machynlleth, one of the men grumbles that this has been the most chaste raid he has ever been on; "murderously so," his friend says. And the grumble catches on until the men sing a song of the virgin army, replacing "Mary". They march on to the power centre that carries more weight than its humble size. The march quickly over the rough terrain towards the town, the centre will move first to take the town, leaving the command position free to manoeuvre. They ford the river with ease and come upon a town emptied of people. The scouts kick their mounts on, pushing past the mass of infantry.

"Hurry, hurry across. Form up, form up, hurry now." The men hustle through the ford and on towards the floodplain flanked by wooded hills. The scouts return quickly.

"There's movement in the hills, looks like a lot of men," one of them notes. Harold and Leofwyn kick their mounts and ride with their bodyguard on towards the valley mouth. It has been relatively dry and the ground is firm before their horses' feet. Up ahead on the valley sides are men, thousands of them, forming on the side of the valley. It looks like there are men in the woods too by the swaying of the trees on this calm day.

"Time to flee for the only time today," says Harold drily. They turn back and gallop rejoin their army.

"He actually surprised us," says Harold.

"Good thing we didn't send the scouts out," Gyrth notes.

"So, you hoped he would catch us out, and now we got caught out, you're happy," Edwin asks.

"Something like that."

"How do you feel about killing your brother-in-law, Edwin," Gyrth asks pointedly.

"Much better than you would feel about killing yours."

"Fair enough."

They hurry the men on across the green valley floor towards the slope and face at an angle. They are spread across just over half a mile of the slope, their helmets and shields covering the armour and halberds of the experienced thegns and fyrd, bolstered by Alfred and core groups of Wessex and east Anglian housecarls who are placed to direct the others in formation. Four lines deep, with the usual axe men in the fourth row for now row behind two lines of shield bearing men and missile troops. For an uphill assault the archers and slingers will not be risked unnecessarily but stand behind the first row. They are vulnerable downslope to Welsh archers and slingers and have no resistance to a charge. The rear guard are positioned to face some thirty paces backwards towards the trees and bolstered by the King's guard.

Harold, Tostig and his core group of housecarls stand centre-left. They are mounted still to get a better view of the battlefield ahead. The Welsh are drawn up into five lines across the slope, with their missile troops ahead. Their king is hardly visible higher up on the slopes behind his men. Tostig and his guard ride over, joined again by Morcar. Gyrth is left to supervise the right and centre as they face the men up to make the journey.

"It's an ugly prospect," notes Tostig.

"They have the advantage over our archers – but overshooting a fast-marching group is highly likely," Harold has his helmet perched on the brow of his head, as servants hustle around them bringing ale and wineskins. Harold's boys are with him for now but will be sent to the rear under guard until their time comes.

"It looks like they'll stand and fight, Edwin notes sourly."

"I'm thinking a feigned retreat," Tostig says.

"Risky but possible if we use the right men. Let's avoid unnecessary waste."

"Perhaps a Ralph charge. Led by Ralph," Stanboda, the usually taciturn thegn suggests.

"Ponies might do it but we'd lose a lot and retreating downhill can be dangerous."

In the end they position the army on the flats with the disciplined first rank and archers tasked with the first ascent. The slope is gentle for the first thirty yards or so before reaching a sharper angle.

Up on the slopes the hills, Gryffud, High King of the Welsh, stocky and ram-haired, surveys the English. With him are his half-brothers Bleddyn and Rhiwallon ap Cynfyn, and his son Maredudd. There are the English with their shining helmets and painted and bare shields. Many round, many Kite shaped in the French style, mostly in the front ranks. Rows of spears for half a mile or more.

"This is an interesting formation for sure," says Bleddyn.

"They're going to charge most likely. It's the Saxon way."

"I thought standing still was the Saxon way," Maredudd scoffs.

"We caught them out. But this will be a hard fight. These men are well-armoured and they have Harold. He almost got me last time, boys."

"What do we do, brother," Rhiwallon asks, his gold chains and hair around his temples glistening in the faint mists rolling about them.

"Stand and harry. Keep the archers out front and have them fan out on the wings as the English move up. Simple. Then we can hit them from the rear."

"They're expecting that."

"But not in the numbers we have there. Then we charge. I need this."

"You're telling us. Do we mass on the English left?"

They watch as the horsemen with their finely decorated helmets dismount and the English horses are led off.

"Killing Harold leaves us with his brothers. They're all almost as good. No, we'll play it by ear."

"I wonder who among us will stand though."

"It's tough to say now, after Rhuddlan. No matter. All we have to do is hold until nightfall and we can keep the high ground."

Gryffud rubs his lustrous beard, medium length like his hair, giving him even more of a ram-like look. He walks down towards the front lines, his bodyguard and lords around him. Up to the left and right, fine Lords of Gwynned stand, hedging their bets on the first contact.

* * *

The English kneel and pray in front of their bishops, whose vestments are draped over their mail, their leaders in front of the lines of men. In a wyrd synchronicity, the Welsh kneel at the same time and these men go through the same motions with their respective holy men. Harold places his fist against his brow as he kneels. Beside him are Leofwyn and his bodyguard. His brothers and the Mercians will be doing the same. Then, at the benediction, the Welsh and English all rise as one. There is a light drizzle, but nothing to impact the archers' draw.

Harold has called for more bows to go to the Housecarls in the fourth rank; they are prepping their weapons, boys and servants ready to bring arrows and ale to the ranks. He calls for the horn to be blown. Runners are kept at the ready to meet the other commanders behind the line. Ahead of them, the front line begins to move up the grassy slope followed by a mass of missile troops and backups for the downed, almost crouched behind the shield-bearing spearmen. Ahead of them, line upon line of Welsh spearmen. Round shields and rough clothes, with their lords bedecked in gold. The first arrows come from up the slope and thud into the ground ahead of them. They proceed up the hill, the occasional arrow thudding into a shield. The English bows are still, the men almost creeping along the half mile and housecarls shout orders to the men beside them. Alfred is there in the shield wall, and Gyrth has taken his own position just

The Welsh Campaign

behind the centre left of the first line with his men about him. Tostig, itching for a fight remains with his men, as does Harold, who has no illusions about the fighting to be done. Ansgar has been sent up with Morcar, while Edwin, again, holds the rear.

The Welsh hold. There is no use charging down yet, and the English are not assaulting as one. Gryffud has assumed they spotted his men in the trees and are keeping their forces close in case of retreat. Probably feeling out the lines too. Then the third and fourth ranks begin to move forward a step, one great half mile silver step.

"What's going on," his son asks him?

The first line begins to jog a little forward. On the left are Eadric, Edwin, Thorkel, Ulf and Valdemar, other from Wessex and the King's guard, yelling encouragement to the Fyrd and signalling to each other.

"They think we're soft," says Bleddyn.

"We should charge them," Rhiwallon offers.

"Wait boys. Just wait." Gryffud has one of his men bring a torch up and wave it in a prearranged pattern.

The English line jogs forward and the front ranks of the Welsh stiffen. They are three rows deep, their archers in front, loosing arrows at the English, who keep their formation tight. Here and there a man drops, caught by a lucky arrow, and he is dragged down the slope by his fellows behind, his spot filled by another man. The English continue to a faster run.

"By god, they're going to charge us," Bleddyn says.

The third and fourth ranks of the English move forward one pace again, now yards behind the men in front.

There are murmurs from the men around Gryffud, and he looks down at the English lines, just as they step forward again.

The front rank quickens. The bristling wall of Welsh spears begins to quiver as the English close the gap. Spears are ready behind shields in the looser formation these fighter prefer. The drizzle has stopped now, and small rays of light poke out. The tension mounts as the men brace for impact.

Then the English stop.

"Kneel!" A voice from the left cries out. The front-rank drops behind its shields and a wave of arrows and stones ascend into the mass of Welsh archers in front of them. Some English missile troops have moved out to the wings to aim at the men assembled there.

"Have them fall back," Gryffud yells. A horn is sounded, and the archers high-tail it back behind the wall.

"Stand!" The front-rank stands and they jog another few paces.

"Kneel!" They are now aiming at the legs of the Welsh ranks who have their shields high to take the stray arrows they assume are going to fly overhead. Men go down shouting. The first rank lower shields to cover their legs. Most arrows fly harmlessly over, but some begin to find necks and eyes, and begin to thud into the ranks above their heads. This proceeds apace, with Welsh slingers interspersed among their spearmen timing their shots to hit the English troops below. An English archer goes down with his eye socket caved in and his screams are sickening. Some of the front line of Welsh are starting to get restless with this battle of slow attrition. The third and fourth lines start to jog up the slopes. As the Welsh begin to fall in ones and twos, they spot the remaining English begin the ascent at a jog.

"They're going to charge us!" The cry goes up among the Welsh troops assembled and a mass on the right breaks ranks and charges straight down the hill towards the English line.

"Kneel!" The cry goes up. Another wave of arrows flies into the charging men.

A horn sounds in the distance, as more Welsh break ranks and charge before the English can assemble.

"Archers back!"

The English front line rises to take the first Welsh assault. In scattered attacks, the Welsh slash into the English line, shield upon shield. Spears stab into faces and necks, and the Welsh fall with barely a movement in the English line. Gyrth is stabbing furiously into the soft parts beneath the helmets.

Gryffud calls for a general assault, now that they have lost order. Then men begin to move.

The English fourth ranks turn and jog back down the slope, as the archers flee. Then the first line moves backwards, slowly managing their descent. Some men trip and fall, but they are hauled back up and dragged along. The Welsh begin to descend, and the half-mile of English, having dealt with the first assault, turn, and flee as quickly as they can. Downslope, the third rank is moving backwards slowly, stopping to gauge the retreat, before moving back again. The finely armoured warriors on the left and right are up behind their shield wall, gauging the retreat. The shield wall parts for the archers, who race breathless behind them. Then the line of shields itself turns and heads back down the slopes, further onto the flats of the valley bottom. They form up again as their countrymen run like hell down to the valley floor, pursued by the Welsh forces. It is a close thing. Gyrth and his men on the left are almost caught up with by a pursuing knot of Welsh spearmen. Arrows and spears are loosed at the fleeing rank and men, mostly unarmoured fyrd, go down, their yells and screams encouraging their countrymen to even faster descents.

Every man of the third line is angled slightly to the right as their countrymen break down onto the flats and rush past them. The stragglers are encouraged as they huff down the slope fighting for every breath. Then the line closes, and the first rank locks in behind the third, switching positions. There is some thirty feet between the slops and the shield wall now and wave upon wave of arrows are fired into the approaching Welsh army, hurtling down to the valley bottom. Some trip over the English fallen, tumbling down the slopes and causing further obstacles, others go down clutching at necks and groins as the English arrows find their targets. Still, they come on, a mass of spears and shields headed straight for the shields arrayed in front of them. The murderous rain of arrows continues, smacking into shields and men.

Upslope, Gryffud, readying his guard, has the signal flame waved again. After an age dull smudge of orange appears faintly among the trees in the distance. He lets out a deep breath. Raising his sword and shield above his head he gives a roar and begins his charge down the slopes towards the English lines.

* * *

The feint worked. Harold takes his place back in the command position, stepping up on a small block to survey the approaching horde. Off in the distance he sees rows of the enemy immobile on the wings. He steps back down, slamming his helmet back on his head and gives orders to the runners to have the fourth rank cease firing and gather their axes. The stacked dead before them are significant enough to slow the charge, as men speeding trip over the slope and others slow to negotiate the fallen. The result is a scattered front. Many of the English dead and wounded have been recovered, dragged downhill by their fleeing mates and carted off towards the baggage train where the captive healers wait under the watchful eyes of Fyrd. The rest they will have to dig out at the end.

The First wave slams into the front rank of English shields. The second rank, still a little winded, pushes up against them like a stack or wood props, the men in both rows angled slightly with their left feet forward and their right dug in to absorb the shock. The archers and slingers are firing at a higher angle now, arrows looping up and down over the wall. Up come the housecarls, some three to four feet apart, wide enough for them to swing their axes up and over the lines of men. Their momentum slowed by the dead and the flat ground ahead of their enemy, the Welsh slam into the shields, hacking with swords and stabbing with spears. Then the axes swing over the wall, shields are hooked by one man, while another slashes down on a neck. Men in the front ranks flinch as blood spurts over their faces, but they stand in a tight formation, wedged together. A man of the fyrd is caught in his eye and lets out a scream, he writhes to break free of the wall but strong arms behind him holds him in place until the pressure eases in that place. In the centre the men of Mercia are hard at it, in their portion of the half mile. Axes are swung hard between the gaps of the helmets and shields, around the housecarl's head and down in an arc. This pattern is played out down the half mile of war as the runners track back and forth. There, on the right, a break in the line and a group of Welsh pouring through. Tostig hurls himself towards the breach along with his bodyguard, yelling to the Northumbrians to get their lines faced as he carves his axe through a triumphant looking Welsh swordsman. They have to move fast, slashing and hacking while a group brace behind their shields and try to push the enemy back to plug the breach. The ground is becoming slippy with muck and blood but he maintains his footing as he cuts his way through. On each side his men brace the walls of men as others haul fyrd and housecarls both into place. It's a messy thing, men faltering under the pressure, a fyrdsman on the left trying to defend against slashes while holding his place goes down and is hauled back. The gap widens, so Tostig barrels through, screaming for his men to follow. They are out into the mass coming towards them, spreading out to wield their axes in sweeping arcs down on men's necks, or slicing legs and groins in an upwards arc. Almost all are in simple breeches and there is nothing to stop the butchery. Some in the wall start to come out but are held back into position by calmer heads. Some sixty of his guard have come through and begin their work, making a clearing with their sweeping axes.

From his vantage point, Harold can see the end of the Welsh lines coming down the slopes. Off on the wings, the rest of the army of Gwynned stands immobile. A runner makes it from Tostig's position and notifies him of the breach. As he steps down, an arrow whistles past his face and thuds into the man behind him. He turns, looking for the victim, who has fallen back with an arrow in his shoulder. The man is dragged off cursing that he hasn't seen any action yet. So far, the line on the left his holding and housecarls are positioned to fend off any flanking attacks, hunkered down behind shields they will discard as soon as the fighting starts. He is with his core bodyguard, the rest spread out as axes or bolstering the wall. Olaf, Hereward, and Wulfstan tight against him with Leofwyn close by to act as a second. The dead and wounded are dragged by as Harold seeks direction from the movement of men along the line. Behind them, the baying of horns.

They turn as a group to see another army streaming down the forested hill to their rear, as expected. The wings on the upper slope still do not move as the momentum of the enemy force begins to slow on the left wing. Harold orders his man to give the signal for a general attack. The horn blows three times and is picked up down the half mile in a delayed burst of sound above the fray. He and his men take shields as the lines begin to move forward.

"Halfdan," he shouts above the metal rage, "go to the rear and bring the boys. You – signal for the horses. Archers to the rear!"

Another horn blast goes up as the Earl and his bodyguard deal with some enterprising Welsh who have made a detour around to the wings. Spears are hurled at the enemy to break their attack, then the spearmen draw their hand axes, daggers or swords. Harold and his men charge through the lines, pushing men apart and ordering them forward. Shields first hard into the enemy. He can feel Leofwyn on his right hurling his shield at a group in front on them, then the arc of an axe and his own shield battered. Gyrth is yelling instructions to the men of East Anglia. His bodyguard spread out through the breaks in the lines as the second line pushes past the first and the whole English front runs forward. Tired men at the back now. Spears are hurled again and a rain of arrows falls in front of them, in a mass of agony. The Welsh are still hitting hard as they run and Harold wields his Dane axe one handed as he breaks through the Welsh mass into the thick of it. He can hear Hereward and Olaf timing their blows together, Cyneweard screaming insults and Harold the Dane cursing the Welsh in his native tongue. All manner of curses in English and Welsh, screaming and the pitch of blood out of wounds. And the dent of weapons on mail and helmets. Then he too launches his shield at the legs of a group of men and glances around in the haze of battle to make sure he is clear. The first swing, then the second, high and low. Clearing the decks. All around them men falling, culled beneath the finer blades and armour of the English. A man next to him down, he swings at the attacker and grabs him up. Oswald. Still clutching his axe. Oswald beats his hand on his Lord and charges again. Behind them the old wall coming in strong in pairs and threes, finishing off the wounded and racing into the thick of the attacking throng. It is hard going.

Off on the right Tostig and his men are surrounded, forming a half-moon to defend themselves. Stanboda and Bradan are with him, as is old Aethelgar, who is as bloody with a shield and hand axe as the Dane Axe butchers around him. Men falling around him, shields cracking, noses breaking and the crunch of the butcher's work everywhere. On the general advance signal, the Northumbrians smash through the encircling Welsh and beat a path forward. Here and there, the enemy begin to run back up the hill. Off to the right, a group in fine armour hacking at the Northumbrian Fyrd who have charged ahead at the signal. The press is too great here for Tostig to break off and meet with that group. He rages in frustration and begins hacking at one of the enemy, then he too is off in a frenzy followed by his bodyguard, yelling and screaming at the enemy. His army is with him now and he yells support as they make their way towards the slope. The Northern army is behind him, and now with him, and they begin to press on.

In the centre, the Mercians are hard pressed by enemy forces coalescing down the slopes. Still maintaining their formation, interlinked with the men of East Anglia and Wessex to their left and the Northumbrians to their right, they are starting to buckle. Housecarls, swinging axes are finding their targets but are as often having to shove the men in front back into shape; Edwin himself has pushed up against the wall more than once, and sends a runner to Harold just as the order to attack begins. He stretches an arm to stop the runner, but the boy is gone, his wrapless breeches flapping against his calves.

"How are we supposed to attack," he yells to one of his thegns. The thegn shakes his head and looks at the encroaching Welsh begin to gather momentum.

On his own left, Gryffud is fighting hard with his bodyguard and brothers beside him. They have pushed to the front and are dodging blows as the English advance, breaking formation and offering themselves to his sword. He yells for his signaller to sound the order for the wings to attack, and the great horn blows. He glances back, and up on the slopes, the wings are motionless. He orders the horn blown again while cutting into a Northumbrian neck.

At the rear, as archers begin to flow towards them, across the beaten ground, Morcar and Ansgar have their men faced up in a tighter formation. There are Welsh warriors streaming down the slopes.

"We could get overrun," Ansgar says. "Fucking Godwins." Morcar stares hard at him. Off in the near distance, the noise of battle is thunderous.

"We should see to the wings, let's get as many of the housecarls as we can afford protecting our flanks." Morcar nods and gives the order to the warriors about him. They will be spread thin.

"Harold sent us archers," the young man notes.

"He should have sent us thegns."

The Welsh continue their descent through the woods and thicket, swords and spears held by their sides as they negotiate their way.

Harold is cutting his way through the Welsh ranks, Gyrth bellowing beside him and Leofwyn making his own quiet way through the masses. His bodyguard are spread out with Gyrth's, making a lopsided force. Half the fyrd are hanging back, out of the threat of axe swings. They take to cleaning up behind the big men in front, murdering and stripping the injured of their armour in the middle of the fight. Then they hear a foreign horn, and another sounding soon after. Some behind the main action stop to look up the grassy slopes to the masses of men on the wings.

Harold keeps on with his bloody arcs, shouting to his men to keep at it, blocking Welsh swords and axes with the shaft of his axe and kicking at shields to loosen defences. Through masses of men they move and hack and fall. After the first few ranks, the quality of fighter falls and men begin to run, rather than face these iron killers. He breaks out, past the last lines, almost onto the slopes and stops for breath. To the right, Gyrth emerges in his gold embossed helmet. And there, to the left the housecarls of Wessex break through,

"Back and to the right," he barks and the who crew turn and begin to fight hard through the stragglers towards the Mercian lines. Arrows start to fly singly from upslope, but he is heedless of them. Leofwyn yells out to him and he nods to himself repeatedly as they push towards the centre.

The strange horn sounds again.

The centre is about to buckle, the taunts coming hard from the Welsh among the clashing and cracking around them. Edwin mounts his shield and draws his sword, preparing to charge the breach. Then the front line moves forward. There is noise coming from the left, yelling and raging, and the screams of men become louder. He pushes up on his toes to see what is happening. The banner of Wessex is flying just above the men's heads as the whole line begins to peel off into the midst of the Welsh. The fight continues as the strange horn sounds. Up on the slopes, he sees the wings begin to thin. And then as of some trick, the dark patches lighten to green as the Welsh reserves merge into the mountain.

The English reserve are bracing for the fight. Harold's boys have been snatched up and are lashing out at the Housecarls who shepherd them to the front.

"You'll get a fight lads," one of the men is heard saying as the boys curse at him.

The Welsh stream down, their weapons dull under the clouds. Until another horn sounds. And the attack stops still. The occasional man blunders down on top of his mates, but some sixty yards from the English line, the mass turns and heads back into the wooded slopes.

"What just happened?" Morcar is speechless.

"Damned if I know," Ansgar says.

A frustrated Housecarl hurls his axe at the retreating forces.

Over on the front, Gryffud is being shoved back up the hill by his bodyguard.

"The bastards!" He is beside himself.

"Brother, we must flee. We still have our reserves. All is not lost."

And so, the High King of the Welsh is manhandled off the battlefield as the horn sounds the retreat. All around him, his army leaves the field.

*   *   *

Eventually the three English leaders meet in the centre of the battlefield. All around them, the dead and injured, one man still crawling towards them with his legs sawn off below the knee is mercifully dispatched by Gyrth, much to the chagrin of his bodyguard who were placing bets on how far the wretch could crawl; his sword still clutched in his hand.

"By god, brother, you've turned red," Gyrth notes as Tostig approaches them.

"I lost my helmet somewhere back there," he says. "That was quite the fight."

"So, your men had your back – who would have thought it," his younger brother claps him on the shoulder and grins.

"What the hell happened," Edwin is rubbing at his wrists, sore from unfamiliar hard fighting.

"Some fine Welsh Lords decided that today wasn't Gryffud's day," Harold replies. "Every man has his reckoning."

"We were hard-pressed Harold." Edwin stares hard at the big man, bloodied yet still hale.

"What my brother means to say is thank you," Morcar says.

"It was a good fight for sure. I had plans for the horses," Harold stares into the distance for a few moments.

"Good plans, then Harold, I'm glad." Gyrth laughs and calls for ale. Englishmen who have had their take begin to sit against their hauls on the slope as others strip the dead across the battlefield.

"I was fearing we would be overrun on those back slopes," Morcar muses.

"That's what the horses were for," Harold draws his lips in.

"I saw him," Tostig shakes his head, every small crease on his face made deeper by the thick layer of dried blood, as if an ancient carving of himself. "Gryffud."

"He's done."

"What now then?" All along the battle lines the English dead are being dragged and hauled into carts and the wounded transported carefully. Of Harold's guard, seven are dead and the same badly wounded. The Mercians and Northumbrians have taken the brunt of the casualties, although their numbers are slight compared to the Welsh. Where the line did not hold, Tostig and his housecarls reacted quickly enough to stem the bleeding. Edwin, unused to combat seems perplexed.

"We carry on," says Harold flatly. "After I bathe, obviously."

* * *

Gryffud sits with his half-brothers and his son.

"We'll split up," he says. "If anything happens to me, strike a deal with Harold."

"You think he'll talk after all this?"

"He has no desire for Wales. If only…never mind. We are where we are, brothers."

"What of Maredudd?"

"He goes with you—no arguing boy. What is the point of all…this…without an heir? Take the boy. I'll head Northwest and see what I can rustle up."

They clap each other on the back as they hug. Then his brothers take their leave and ride off into the hills, leaving him with his guard and the men still left loyal to him. As for the rest, they are gone back to their fiefdoms, ready to treat with the Godwinsons and make their soft beds. He looks around at the wall of dejection.

"Cheer up boys, it could be worse: you could have just lost a kingdom."

*

For the next month, English forces continue to harry Wales; though, where messengers come, Harold is happy to treat with local kings. They press on with cavalry raids as the army moves up a few miles a day. The land army protect the supply lines as the Godwin brothers raid on horseback, Tostig happy to be on the move and fighting again. Word comes that the King has moved to Gloucester with his retinue. At the end of spring, as Harold and his army camp, a retinue of finely dressed men come towards them.

Harold emerges from his tent in a tunic, strapping on his sword. He is clean and well-groomed in these days of hunting and raiding. The retinue is stopped by guard far beyond the picket lines, but he is nevertheless surrounded by his men. His Goshawk sits on its perch.

"Maybe later," he says to it mildly and strides towards the strangers.

"This is good country. Verdant, beautiful."

"Thinking of staying, Earl Harold," the men have dismounted, and their leader, small and wiry, moves to shake hands with him.

"Not on your life," he laughs. The man translates to his companions who smile in unison. With a companiable gait, they move to the command tent, where Harold stands in front of the map table with his brothers and the earls and thegns arrayed about him in their fine dress.

"We come bearing a gift for you and your King," the leader, Llewellyn, states flatly.

One of the men is carrying a small chest.

"Is that what I think it is," Edwin looks down as he eyes the chest.

Harold makes way for the man, who has a serious look about him. The man puts the chest down and flips the clasp. There, the bearded head of Gryffud, High King of the Welsh, sits among fragrant herbs.

"He's remarkably well preserved, your brother," Gyrth notes to Edwin, who is blanched against his blue tunic.

"We took care of him…after," Lewellyn says.

"After you gutted and flayed him alive," Leofwyn looks hard at the Welsh. He has recovered men in this state.

"We made it quick. No use making a martyr of the man. Besides, he has a long journey to—Winchester, is it?"

"Gloucester actually," Harold notes, taking one last look at his enemy before shutting the casket and motioning to a servant to take the head away.

"Was he read the last rites," Bishop Ealdred asks with a furrowed brow.

"Under the circumstances, no."

"And…his body?"

"Buried, with honour."

"But not Christian rites."

"I would say not."

"A pity for a king to die in such a way."

"He made his bed, bishop."

"Have a mass for him, then, Bishop," Harold says.

"So that's it then," Athelgar says.

"For now, yes. There is the matter of the succession—the Welsh succession."

"We have our man," Lewellyn says.

"Edward will want a prince of the blood.

"Half of Wales are princes of the blood, Earl Harold, Rhodri pipes up.

"We need a clean slate," the Welsh leader says plainly.

"Edward will want his own choice, and he'll demand fealty."

"And what of you Earl Harold?"

"I want peace on our border; the king will have his wish—you should all resign yourselves to Gryffud's half-brothers."

"Wales divided again."

"It was always thus," Tostig notes. Men turn to look when he speaks and a half smiles plays on Harold's lips; he meets his brother's eyes.

"A divided Wales, a united England, perhaps. No matter. I thank you for the gift and would ask that you accompany us to Wales and have the brothers—"

"Bleddyn and Rhiwallon."

"Yes, them—sent to Gloucester to treat with the King."

"And what of the boy?"

"He is of no concern to me. Come now, let us drink together and talk of hunting and your bows. They make for fine weapons but I doubt most Englishmen could draw one."

Harold takes Lewellyn by the arm and they make towards the kitchens to organize the feast.

"That's it," says Tostig to Athelgar, who beats his lord on his chest with a wide grin.

"Bless you, lord; you have returned to us."

"Perhaps reforged," Tostig smiles. He and his brothers leave the tent together and follow after Harold.

*

At Gloucester, Edward is delighted at the presentation of the finely preserved head, and heaps praise on the Godwinson brothers. At the great feast, which takes over the town, Tostig sits at the king's left hand as Queen Edith is relegated to a place below her brother, and she sits with a frown, eying her brother jealously. The princely Welsh lords have paid their homage to Edward in exchange for autonomy, and they are given places down from Harold, who takes pains to rise and make pleasantries with them.

"I am aware that if the Welsh had the heart for it, our path would have been more dangerous," Harold says to them. They smile at the diplomacy and raise their cups to this contradiction of a man. As happy with a treaty as a hard fight. The days pass with hunting and feasting, but nary a word or mockery of the Welsh. Harold himself takes two stags to Tostig's three and upstages the king once more with his goshawk. All this delights the blithe King, whose border is secure and coffers full of Welsh tribute.

One evening as Harold walks outside to get air away from the smoke and odours of the feast, Edwin catches up with him. Harold gives him a friendly nod.

"Harold, why did we go to war with Gryffud. Really?"

"The succession," Harold says flatly.

"But there must be more…there is. Your exile, perhaps?"

"It is late to take revenge for what happened to us."

"Late, but perhaps just."

"And you, Edwin. Your brother-in-law is dead. Your sister widowed."

"And my life is made less complicated. Father is sick. I will inherit a less fraught political landscape now."

"I look forward to a fruitful relationship, Earl Edwin," Harold smiles gently. "Perhaps in a year we will have a lasting peace again."

"The succession?"

"Yes."

Edwin shakes his head.

The Oath, 1064

It has been a year since the campaign in Wales. The earl is, for the most part, splitting his time between Bosham and Winchester. King Edward, having built a new cathedral at Westminster, is spending more time in London, coming to Wessex for hunting and the occasional feast, and leaving the running of his kingdom to the first Earl. One week Edward even comes to Bosham and eats with the family in their private hall, bringing his queen back to her family home. The king has not yet paid his tithes to time, and he is as hale and blithe as a young man still. Harold's nightwalking has lessened since his war has ended, much to the relief of his bodyguard, who lose years from their faces and contemplate wives. The Queen in private warns Harold of increasing interest in Edward's health by William, Duke of Normandy: a man he has yet to spend much time with. In response, he pulls her hair and she chases him around the room with a brush. Still Harold makes no firm move to secure the succession for Edgar Atheling or any other. Edith has given birth to another son, Ulf, and they fret about finally sending a boy to the priesthood.

"A bishop in the family would be a wise move," Edward notes. Harold laughs at this.

"We already have one, lord. His name is Tostig."

"Tosty the bloody, now."

"He has fire again, that one."

Leofwyn rotates between his new lands and Bosham now, his own brood growing. Gyrth is content in Essex, making merry of Lady Richeldis and turning a fine trade with Dane and Flem alike.

And Tostig is in the North, with a new fire in him, and new orders from his king.

The older boys are blooded now and divide their time between the warriors and their books, learning their languages and arithmetic and even traveling to Flanders to watch the merchants trade. Magnus is a constant at his side, learning his trade and gaining first-hand knowledge of the affairs of state. Treaties are signed between the Welsh princely brothers and each of the Earls, and a new series of stables are founded up Watling Street to allow for rapid troop movements within England. The Normans, hardly a presence in these last years, pay more visits to Winchester to sound out this Earl, but, as often, go straight to Edward in Westminster and regale him with tales of the hero Duke's prowess. At one point the Queen makes light of this and asks if William himself attacked a castle with a handful of men and sent the French king packing. Harold's name is on the lips of many. His intentions are opaque, and the French cannot believe that such a man has no ambitions on the throne. Edith's answer as always:

"He is content to be first among the lords and the strongest of men. Who needs civil war when you can be the realm's protector?"

There will be no campaign against the Scots yet; Tostig or his lickspittle Copsig may have warned Malcom of Harold's intent, as word of border raids are few. So be it, a time for peace, trade, and the shoring up of English defences. Few dare to pull the wool over this man's eyes; literate in English and Latin, he is diligent and canny, and the King's purse fattens with as the graft is caught with a knowing wink and a pleasant warning. But it is Bosham that has his heart. Bosham, where his family lie and his men surround him, loyal always.

"Missing Leofwyn, Earl Harold," Olaf asks one day as they go out on the downs hawking with three local thegns, all mates of his youth. He has a distant gaze on that tan face, expressions that flit between affection and sorrow. The thegns are more formal with him now, only slightly so, but enough to lose his comfortable familiarity. They laugh a little too hard at his jokes and he catches their awed attention out of the corner of his eye. It irks the Wessex boy in him. But his men more than make up for his friends' courtesy.

"Yes, and Wulfnoth."

"Your brother, lord? He's been gone some 15 years or more."

"I know," the thegns nod sympathetically. "All these years appeasing the King; all my power here and it's not worth a shilling in Normandy."

"I wouldn't turn my nose up at a shilling, lord," Hereward cuts in.

The group goes silent.

"You have left it long. Perhaps when the King passes…" Ulfwith, almost as large as Harold though with a look of contented gluttony, notes. "Perhaps you could just write a letter to that Duke William, Harold."

"I hear he is illiterate."

"He's a bastard too."

"I've never met the man, and I've met half of Normandy with their constant shuttling."

"Your father really got them, Harold."

"Ha! Yes, he really did, didn't he?"

"Here today…"

"He was snatched, you know, by Robert of... Ju-mieges, while the rest of us were hurrying away with our ships and our gold."

"But it was Edward, Harold."

"In a temper, yes.

"Still, he is an old man now. It may turn out you can get him back."

"Truth be told, I have not asked for fear of raking up the dead. Look at that viper, cunning little bastard." Harold's goshawk appears from behind a tree and snatches a young rabbit.

"They're like flying weasels, those goshawks."

"They're not fucking weasels, Hereward. Don't you have a sector to guard?"

"I'll go do my rounds, then, lord."

"Yes, you do that." He can't help but smile at the tall lean guard, as he kicks his horse off further into the downs, with Olaf muttering at him. "There are few men as wicked with an axe as those two."

"Or as lacking in sense," Wulfstan states.

Clouds shift and the sun seems to dart as shadows roam the downs so rapidly it seems time itself is running faster.

"I feel like chasing other hunting grounds. Perhaps some fishing too. When the boys get back, let's put a gang together."

The group catch up to their Earl as he is leaning in talking closely to a sailor on his Byrding, his hand clamped on the man's shoulder. The man is nodding furiously.

"We're taking a Byrding, then?"

The Oath, 1064

"Yes. There's nothing to fear."

"Let's have some coast guard along too", Wulfstan says, as a team of servants carry food and wine onto the ship. A couple of men also carry a chest, half staggering onto the gently rocking vessel.

"Fine," the Earl nods, gazing out at the clouds still in their crazy race through the sky. "Odd clouds these. Like they're drunk."

"Or restless, lord. The Earl's clouds, I think they call them."

"Oh, do they?"

"Where's the little one today?"

"He's with the priest learning his letters. Best leave him to it."

"Right you are, Harold."

There are eleven of them: Ulfwith, Algar, thegn, Olaf, Hereward, Wulfstan, and Harold, plus two men at the sail, a man at the rudder and two servants, one with a hound and one a falconer. They board close to the house at Bosham, locals bidding good morning to the Earl. The occasional "Morning Harold," makes him beam. Then he collects himself. The day is dull and overcast, but no threat of wind or rain as yet. Rank among the warriors and thegns is all but gone on board and they laugh and draw breath at Hereward's sheer lack of deference to his lord. Harold is all smiles on board and shares his bread with the sailors and servants both, batting the hound around his ears and appraising this new hawk.

"Not taking the favourite, lord."

"No, I have to get this new one right. Shit I forgot about the rest of you. Hurry there, Theodred and get another hawk for the boys. Otherwise, they'll be watching me all damned day."

They finally push off and set the boat on its course further out to sea than usual, so Harold can fish for bass and pollock. They will move to the Isle of Wight in the afternoon and watch the goshawks. From there, perhaps east where Harold can see to his lands for a day or so, while catching the sights. Three warships follow at a polite distance, fully crewed. They push out into the channel, where, judging some sign, Harold has them stop. There, they throw their lines out to sea, along with a large net that trawls behind the boat, waiting for its catch. They spend the morning thus, lines tugging and the happy successes and failures of their fishing filling them up with life. The hawks fuss at the rocking of the boat and the dog is sick, but no one pays them any mind as they bring in a cod large enough to feed half the crew aboard. The sea rocks the boat a little heavily and sends Algar down.

"Good thing we didn't bring you to Rhuddlan, Algar."

"Yes, Harold," he chuckles dutifully.

As the sun lopes overhead, just barely lighting the clouds, the wind picks up.

"Fuck," Wulfric mutters at the cloud pattern.

"Yes," Harold looks over as the clouds begin to roll like waves across the sky. "We should head east, see if we can beat the storm before the sea swallows us." Then he stopped and stared upwards.

"What lord?"

"It's what I cursed Swein with."

"Well, the pilgrimage swallowed him lord, so you were close," Olaf nods wisely.

"Getting superstitious in your old age, Harold," Algar asks.

"Fuck off, Algar," Harold laughs, and the gap between them closes.

"Boys, turn the sail and see if we can head east. Wigland – hit the rudder hard and snap away from the coast, I don't want us getting driven in. On my mark. Olaf – go help with the sail. Herward—not a smart word from you. Actually, get to the rudder and help – listen to Wigland. Everyone else, get yourselves anchored."

Harold himself runs to the sail to help with the timing of the turn. The winds start to whip gravel against their faces, and the hound cries balefully.

"Make sure the hawks are tied down." The falconer dutifully crouch-hops across the deck and binds the hawks to himself before coiling a rope around his waist.

The rain and the win begin to lash them until the wind picks the sail and sends the ship off on a crazy tangent. Wigland is almost thrown as a wave crashes over the deck, soaking the fine clothes of the nobles and the dun clothes alike of the servants.

"Furl the sail, we'll just go round in a circle if we try to outrun it!" Harold's voice carries well through the impending gale.

Hereward is at the rudder with the sailor, using all his might to keep the thing from snapping back against the side of the boat. Olaf helps to furl the sail, so the ship doesn't head off in a wild arc onto some rocks. The rain is beating down now and lightning cracks against the sky. Waves come on harder and higher until the ship is wrenched upwards and away from shore. The coast guard ships are lost to sight as the ship heads off on whatever course the sea has chosen for it.

"Hold on lads. We're not lost yet!"

"It's not our first storm, lord," yells Olaf.

"No, but it may be our last," yells Hereward as a vast wave sweeps towards them.

"Christ have mercy," one of the sailors cries out as the wave throws the ship further and further. The day is dark and the only light serrates the sky in jagged bursts. They grip anything that seems solid in this mass of wind and water and fight to hold on as the storm surges on.

* * *

It is early morning and the storm has passed with no loss of life. Even the hound hung on, wrapped up in the hollow of Ulfwith's body as he clung to the ship. One of the goshawks too is still alive, the other bashed against the starboard side of the hull.

"Well," says Harold, "Does anyone have a clue where we are?"

"Not England, that's for sure," says Hereward, pointing.

Off in the near distance, the coastline does seem unfamiliar.

"It's not France?" Ulfwith looks out, the dog whimpering and nuzzling into him still.

"It does seem that way," Harold seems almost more impressive with the brine in his hair and his clothes tight against his large frame. Except for Olaf, the others are shades above the dog in waterlogged misery.

"Any sign of the coastguard?" They all peer off away from shore.

"So you decided to invade Normandy with a single ship this time," Hereward says after an age of watching. Algar laughs heartily as the others chuckle. "I hear duke William lives in a stone fort, so it may be harder to sneak up on him."

"Fair." The Earl gives a broad smile and points towards the shore. "Well, lads, we've lost our food and there's scant wind in our favour. Let's head towards the shore and see what we can see. At least we have some gold still." A barrel of wine bobs by just out of reach and they watch it go.

"I'd give the gold for that wine," Olaf states.

Harold takes the rudder and orders the sail unfurled. The slight wind catches the sail, and he hauls the rudder to the starboard, turning the ship hard against the waves. The long sands of the bay curve ahead of them, hardly threatening their boat. Then, just to their right of their view, they spy two ships coming out to meet them.

"It's the French," says Ulfwith—"I know the designs."

"Yes, that is the plainest thing but well done. You are first among us to state the obvious today." Hereward cackles and gives the thegn a hard stare when he is shot a look. "We'll get led in. Something tells me we're in for a long day. Let's make sure the last goshawk is fed before we go. I don't want this trip to end in more tragedy."

A mailed figure, growing larger by the moment, raises a gloved hand to the men onboard. Harold meets his gesture. "Olaf, raise the banner, would you?" The big man ties the banner of Wessex to the mast rope and hauls it upwards.

"There, at least they'll see we're not some merchant ship to be seized."

"Now we're a prize."

"Yes, exactly that, Olaf. And a prize lives."

They fetch their swords and axes from the ship's store in the middle of the hull and strap them on.

"Is there time for a shave, Theodred?"

"Perhaps, lord," the servant chuckles nervously.

"I have bad French—Hereward?"

"Yes lord," he says, "Flemish, too, in case we're there."

"I have Norwegian, lord," Olaf is staring at the ship brimming with archers and spearmen. Wulfstan rolls his eyes.

"That will serve us nicely. Right then boys."

"Arête monsieurs!" A voice calls out from the lead ship.

"That means stop," says Hereward.

"That much I know."

"Bonjour," booms Harold, "Je suis Harold, le Duc de Wessex."

"You don't need the "le" in there," Hereward corrects. "But it's good enough."

"Welcome, Duc," the man booms back in a thick French accent. "Ici…here." Pointing to the bay.

"We're in France, then," Algar says.

"Wigland, take us in."

The boat ambles across the waves, flanked by French ships, more cumbersome than the English longships but no less deadly to the men on the boat. They can see archers and men with mechanical bows aimed at them.

"Crossbows, I think they call them. I keep meaning to import some."

"Now's our chance to get a first-hand look," says Wulfstan.

"I played with some in Flanders," Hereward replies. "They're powerful, much more than an English bow, but slow to load." The others nod knowingly while staring at the two ships.

The boat follows the lead ship as it sails ahead of them, its soldiers turned back to face the English in their ship.

"Perhaps we'll get fed," Ulfwith sighs.

"This trip will be good for you," Harold laughs. "Nothing like the soft life to turn a man to fat. Look at those beaches! Large enough to land the entire English fyrd in one go."

They move to the Westerly side of the bay's horseshoe and have the sail tacked. Ahead, on the sands, they see mounted men, some of whom take off at the sight of the boats approaching.

"They came prepared, it seems," Algar notes, rubbing at his stubble.

"Don't be too compliant, Wigland, beach us a little further from where they point us. It will give us time to get off the boats and get ourselves together. Let's be sure not to get up in arms if they manhandle us."

They all nod assent as Wigland steers the boat off to the starboard, much to the anger of the French onboard the nearest longship. They beach with a jarring crash.

"Sorry, Earl Harold. It's the nerves."

The sand is the muddy yellow of English sand, and they deboard, Harold out front with his thegns and Hereward, with Olaf and Wulfstan flanking. The servants and sailors are ordered behind to follow what the French call "protocol".

The riders approach them at a pace, kicking sand up as they halt.

"Nom?"

"Harold, Duc de Wessex."

"Better, lord," whispers Hereward; he raises his hand in annoyance.

The riders look stunned for a moment; the lead, dressed in mail like his men, collects himself and barks something to one of the other riders. They stand facing these men as the rider takes off. Off to their left they hear the beaching of a ship, followed sometime later by the sounds of mailed men headed to them.

"Theodred, do you have the goshawk? And what of that hound?"

"All good," the man stammers.

"Be calm, my man."

"Nous somme prisonniers?" to the rider.

"Non, invitees," the leader says with a smirk. By now they are surrounded by men and the sea.

"This is a warm reception."

"They thought they had a catch and now they have a prize it seems."

"These French are pirates," Ulfwith stands with his earl as if in a line of battle.

"It seems that way."

After an age, horses are brought to them. The French guards size up the men before them and show four horses to Harold, the thegns and Hereward.

"By god Hereward, I took you for a ceorl."

"I am not like these peasants you consort with."

"He got the rest right; well—a thegn you are."

"So, the rest of us walk?"

"Don't rock the boat, Wulfric. Oh, our weapons? They could give a man his sword at least. Hand them over men, that's right, all of you. Here, Theodred, take care of the hawk—non…ce'st mine."

After the weapons are transferred, the Earl and the others mount and are led across to an estuary. Those on foot are treated roughly by the soldiers around them. They travel for a mile or so until they reach a quay, where they are motioned to dismount and board barges. The Englishmen are separated by rank, with housecarls and servants bound behind. Their boat has been pillaged and the soldiers load gold and weapons onto the rear barge with the non-nobles.

Harold and the thegns are offered seats while Hereward attempts to strike up a conversation with the leader, who shrugs at his questions and motions impatiently for him to sit.

"Where are we going, Hereward?"

"A castle, lord; we're in a region called Ponthieu."

"The leader's name is Guy."

"Like every other French bugger," Wiglaf says.

The sands recede behind them and the banks are wide and marshy, giving way to reeds and scattered woodlands.

"Not unlike England," says Ulfwith.

"As if god wrenched the lands apart because we could not agree," says Wiglaf.

"Jesus," Herward mutters to a smile from his lord.

"Perhaps, Duke William might…unite our people," the leader says. "I am Jean."

"It's Jean, or Guy," Hereward notes.

"Jean." The man stares blankly at the warrior who takes no notice of his gaze.

Small boats pass them, minding their own trajectories; under other circumstances this would be a dreamlike passage up the river, oars beating rhythmically under a calm sun, clouds ambling like the sheep dotted around the banks where man has claimed fields from reeds and marshes. Harold leans back and soaks the morning in.

"I could use a bath."

"Later," Jean says. "Enjoy the journey, Duke."

* * *

They sit in the Duke's hall, almost as supplicants for a king's favour. They have been here for two days and the Count has grudgingly provided baths and ordered the men's clothes returned from the pillage of the ship's hold. Guy is of middling height and stocky, his hair cut, like so many others around him, in the Norman style, with the back of his head shaved. He sports a thick moustache and eyes Harold with admiration. He speaks.

"The duke says you are an impressive man, Duke Harold."

"He said he thinks you're handsome, lord," Hereward, still a thegn, whispers.

"I see."

"He wants you to show him your famous…Danish weapon." The English snigger.

"The Dane axe, yes. Have a servant bring our axes."

"Ha! That will not happen monsieur, although the Duke will permit one axe to be brought."

"Come," the Duke motions to Harold.

"Je marche." Harold says. "Just like the old days."

They go out into the courtyard, leaving the stone tower they have been cooped up in. Beyond them, down the slope of the mound the tower is perched on, is the town, with a large market square.

"Vite, Vite!" The count motions to his men. They move down to a courtyard or market square, part of which is maintained as a practice area for the garrison of forty or so. An axe is brought to the Duke who smiles and motions to Harold.

"Show."

"The Duke loves the stories of the English warriors. He has his moustache…"

"Silence Jean! Show." He hands the axe to Harold.

"Moi? Je suis un duc."

"Moi aussi. Show."

Harold rolls his eyes in a show of his own protocol. Then he collects himself. The axe sweeps around and over his head, the great arc of the axe scything from left to right, then under. A great dance begins, sweeping and arcing, blocking, kicking, he even rolls with the grace of a man half his size. The whole motion ends with the axe flung hard at the beam of a market stand where it thuds and quivers into silence. There are gasps and scattered applause from the people around him. He has barely noticed.

"Mon dieu. Ce'st magnifique." Guy motions politely for the axe to be brought and holds it, swinging it gingerly. They all smile and laugh along at his childlike wonder.

"The Duke has never been to England but would like to travel—perhaps to trade."

"He has a trade in noble prisoners from what I hear."

"It is better than murder, my lord. Far better than stealing the ships of the innocent. And do you not trade in men? Women? Children?"

"Fair," says Harold.

"So, we trade in the riche."

The duke is busy testing the edge of the Dane axe when a commotion begins. Armed horsemen are beating their way through the crowd that has formed around the Duke and his hostage Earl. At the front is a mailed man, imposing on his destrier. He has a smooth, blank face, and his eyes betray no emotion. He is erect on his horse and the other men around him look to his every gesture.

"Guy."

"Guillaume." Guy stops in the dirt, his hand on the blade of the axe.

"Pourquoi tien-tu la hache comme ça?"

"Comme ça?"

"Oui."

"Ce'st le Dane axe."

"Oui?"

"Oui, et c'et homme… Il est Harold, Duc de Wessex."

"Oui, Je connais. Relâche-le."

"Mon duc, Il est un grand prix."

"Non, ce'st the Beau-frère de le Roi de l'Angleterre. Relâche-le." Guy nods, his sweaty face marked with disappointment. "Jean, viens avec moi."

Jean, the English speaker, walks up and bows, waiting until the duke motions him to rise.

"This is Guillame, Duke of Normandy."

"I gathered. By God his horse has a large cock."

Jean translates to the Duke; William looks at Harold and mutters something to Jean.

"The Duke says his is as large."

"By the size of his hands, I'd say mine is larger."

The duke's lips twitch and he sets back in his saddle, turning his head and shoulders slightly to the right. After a small age his lip twitches again in a quarter smile and he dismounts nimbly.

"Duc Arold."

"Duke Guillame."

The two men grasp hands, Harold beaming at the blank face.

"You are free," Jean shrugs. "May Duke Guy keep an axe?"

"By all means. And my friends? Mes amis?"

Guy gives a surly nod.

"Oui, les amis aussi," William interrupts.

The others are fetched, angry and unwashed in their captivity. Harold nods gratitude to William, who looks at him.

"The Duke has heard much of your…Wale…"

"Welsh campaign."

"It is good to meet the Duke in person finally. For all the trade and letters we have exchanged."

William raises an eyebrow.

"Alors, nous departons."

"Right then; come on lads."

This time the whole group are given horses. They make their way through a crowd of people, the horsemen around William kicking the peasants out of the way.

"Remind you of anyone," Wiglaf asks.

"Eustace."

After the cold stone tower, the crowded streets and wooden palisades are familiar to the Englishmen, who follow their new host at a distance.

"So are we free or prisoners of a new jailor," asks Wulfric.

"That's an excellent question." Harold is summoned to ride up next to William, who turns his head as he trots up to his host. The surly Jean is brought along to translate between the men; he is a changed man now, eager and nodding energetically. Aside from a few companions, all the men here pay extreme deference to William, who barely acknowledges anyone except a core group. And, now, Harold.

It turns out that William has begun a campaign in Brittany to stamp out a rebellion there. He was at Eu, preparing to sail when he got wind of Harold's arrival.

"The Duke thinks that since you defeated the Britains…you may enjoy defeating their cousins too."

"Ah yes, the Bretons and the Welsh speak a similar language."

"A rare irony, no?"

"Brittany is far."

"We will sail. It is just two days to where our army is."

"How long before we sail?"

"A matter of a day or so."

"My brother…Wulfstan."

"Ah yes, most unfortunate."

"I would like to see him." William shrugs.

"Of course. We will arrange it. He is not far from Eu." Words are exchanged and one of the riders—knights—is sent off at a gallop.

"So it is settled, then? You will fight with our lord?"

"For a time, yes. I must get back to England within the month." Again, William shrugs.

"It is settled, then."

"I like the sound of this lord," Olaf says when he is given word.

"Me too," Herward says. Wulfric simply smiles.

"Are you both joking?"

"No Lord. It's been a while since we had a good fight."

"It's been a year."

"Yes, lord."

"Here we fucking go," Wiglaf booms. The French seem taken aback by this display.

On the way to Eu, they get to know, or know of, William's close companions. His brother, Odo, is at the border with Brittany, supervising the army. Harold and Odo have met before, and this warrior Bishop's ambition and greed are well known. He is garrulous and a good companion at feasts, and the two men conversed in Latin when they met. Stigand and Odo, despite, or perhaps because of, their similarities, despised each other from the offset.

"This is Robert de Mortain, Duc Guillaume's brother, and the man with the dark hair, Guillame FitzOsbern—and there, Roger de

Beaumont, the Duke's...counsellor." The old de Beaumont actually flashes a smile a Harold, who nods a pleasant greeting.

"Les amis."

"Oui, loyal," says William. "Et Vu?"

"I am loyal to my king, make no question of that."

"But you did rebel once, no," Jean translates.

"It was an unfortunate situation."

"Your family against the whole of England. And—Normandy."

"Yes, and we're doing very well thank you."

Jean tells Harold Eustace is with Odo. Harold's face darkens. The French soldiers keenly observe William's reaction. Then he speaks.

"The duke says he would enjoy that fight."

"It would not be much of a fight," Harold says. He does not smile.

"Hm," William utters, his eyes brightening for a moment.

"And what of the King?"

"My brother-in-law is my lord, and I serve him with devotion."

"The Duke asks what your ambitions are?"

"Ambitions? My family have risen from despair to power on more than one occasion. I don't want any more despair, that's for sure. Tell Duke Guillaume my Earldom is my eldest son's inheritance."

The conversation changes to crossbows.

* * *

Eu is a moderate town still under development, a few days' ride from Rouen. Like Guy's fort, this too has a mound with a "keep" on top, much like the hillforts of the Welsh. William explains—through Jean—that they will depart from Le Treport, a short trip down to the coast. Waiting at the keep is his wife, Mathilde. As he dismounts the sheer discrepancy in height causes the English to suppress their laughter. William is tall—taller than Harold, though less broad of back. He stoops and kisses her hand reverently as she peers past him to see these English with their moustaches and long hair.

"Mon épouse," he smiles the rarest of smiles at his introduction. Harold steps forward and gives a French bow to the lady, who offers her hand.

"I've never seen Harold bow to a woman," says Algar.

"But I've seen a lot of women kneel for him," whispers Algar.

"Taking communion is it," asks Hereward, and the thegns splutter, much to the annoyance of their French companions, ordered by rank behind William.

Mathilde takes charge of the conversation, notifying William of troop movements and the passage of supplies to the port. He listens intently, Hereward whispering in Harold's ear.

"The Duchesse is pleased to meet you and your friends Duc Harold, and would like to hear of the King's health."

"He is as hearty as a man thirty years younger," says Harold. She nods at the translation, observing Harold keenly.

"And what of your sister, the Queen?"

"She is at his side, constantly, and content."

"The Duchesse says it is a pity there was no—issue."

"She contents herself with prayer and the running of his household."

William speaks.

"The duchesse will…manage…Normandy in the Duke's absence."

"An exceptional woman." William nods.

"And your wife," asks Jean.

"With child again," Harold smiles.

"The Queen is also blessed with healthy children. She asks what you intend to do with Wales—perhaps you could give your children lands there."

"Intend? Oh, the Welsh will rule themselves and pay us…tribute."

The French seem confused by this response.

"Perhaps the Scots then?"

"Perhaps—our goal is to have a peaceful and secure England."

"The Duchess says you secure peace by conquest, no?"

"And then you spend your life fighting rebellious subjects." William smarts at this. Harold raises his hand in a conciliatory gesture. "Take it from a Godwin." Mathilde smiles and takes the Earl by the hand.

"The Duchess says we have much to learn from each other; much to gain from a renewed friendship."

"The prospect of friendship is one that I look forward to. Increased trade and fair relations would please my King greatly. Now, my…lady, if we could turn to the subject of my brother..."

William interjects.

"He will be brought to you," Jean translates. "After. The Duke excuses himself, but he must talk with his wife and counsellors. Please—make yourselves comfortable. Baths will be arranged. And clothes."

* * *

The journey from Le Treport is uneventful, and the English are allowed to carry their weapons without limitation, much to Olaf's peace of mind. The housecarls and servants are sent to a different part of the boat, while Harold and his thegns are given berths next to William and his close companions. They talk of the raid on Rhuddlan and Harold's early campaigns in Flanders. William's brother talks with quiet awe of his brother's rise to power. William sits and listens quietly to his own tale as Harold leans back and contemplates this man.

* * *

They land without issue near Dol-de-Bretagne at the Mont-St-Miche bay, with its stunning outcrop of rock at the edge of the natural harbour. They disembark amongst the hurried order of a military campaign. Local fishermen and merchants are pushed rudely aside as the Duke and his entourage are met by Odo and a series of. Odo is almost as tall as William, thicker set and quite bald. He spots Harold and grins, dismounting and kissing him on each cheek before hugging him.

"Salve, frater," greetings brother. Harold is happy to see this corrupt yet likeable man—all the more so by acknowledging his avariciousness with glee as he bequeaths gift upon gift to religious establishments to remit his sin. He wears a mace instead of a sword—the only sign that he is a man of the cross; he will bludgeon his foes rather than draw blood. He is dressed in embroidered deep scarlet and is laden with gold chains.

"Et Salve, frater." William looks at him blankly.

"Bonjour, frere." William accepts two kisses and grasps his brother by his shoulders.

From what Harold gathers through the whispering Hereward, the campaign is ready to begin. It is against Conan of Brittany, who has, once again, broken his pledge to William. Harold is led to the Duke's quarters through the muddy streets of Dol-de-Bretagne where he is invited to the map room. William nods as Odo reviews supply and troop routes with the diligence of Gyrth, noting carefully each place name as he points to them, repeating the name each time. It becomes clear the French Duke cannot read and is completely reliant on his brother for such matters.

"So, my letters," Harold begins in Latin.

"Come through me, of course. You English are so particular about your learning."

"It was Alfred who made us read," laughs Harold, "A dream that every Englishman should read and write in his own tongue."

"A literate French peasantry is a dangerous thing. But you English have your slaves, so all your men strut like peacocks. Every man a lord of his...hide. Eo! we talk about the same thing every time, right before we get drunk together."

With the increasingly surly Wulfric and Olaf bunked down with the other men-at-arms, Harold, his thegns—including Hereward, who gives a true translation of the dialogue between William and his coterie—and William's men feast together, Odo pushing for more details of the Rhuddlan raid and subsequent campaign.

"My brother is amazed that you took so few ships and so much risk, to capture this Griffin."

"I have three sons, and four brothers: such a brood can make a man bolder."

"My brother is no stranger to a fight."

"Nor are you, Odo."

"It is a wonder that you do not have a brother of the cloth."

"You sound like Edward."

"Perhaps a son, then. I am useful to my brother in more ways than letters. Having ears and tongues in Rome can help a family's cause. Ah Eustace." Eustace, run slightly to fat but still as proud, enters. He starts when he sees Harold. "I trust you—gentlemen—can be civil."

Harold stands, William watching keenly all the while, his face only slightly relaxed from its usual mask. The rest of the nobility look excited.

"Eustace." The other man looks like a child forced to apologize for misbehaving.

"Duc Harold."

"Ask the Duke if he has made his bed in another man's home recently." Odo claps his hands in delight as French and English lean back to see the reaction. Eustace looks to a man of his who whispers in his ear,

"The Duke hears that you are wont to do this. Although only when his wife is away." There are smiles at this attempt at conciliation.

"I haven't met the Duke's wife yet, though I hear his bed is soft." There is laughter, and Eustace suppresses the urge to step forward.

"Hear this," Odo says in French "Unarmed English against armed French knights. And Eustace sent packing back to Edward." William nods as Eustace bears his humiliation.

Through Jean, who seems to relish his promotion, Eustace speaks again. "The duke was glad to see your family restored to honour and hopes our…families can prosper together."

"Or we can square up and have a fair fight." There is silence at Harold's statement, as he puts his hand on his hatchet. William alone among the French seems eager to see this, leaning forward, his eyes flitting between the two men.

Then Harold laughs, and the tension ghosts from the room. William sits back, a flicker of disappointment crossing his face.

"Alors, mangons," the tall man says.

*   *   *

The next day, the Norman war machine begins to move. Crowds gather to see the army off, which is comprised of more mounted horsemen than the English have seen. Their mail has also been restored to them, polished, although they are given new shields with a Norman brand upon them.

"We're used to these shields," Harold says.

"A good example of how our people thrive together," Odo replies, before translating for his brother's benefit. "Protocol dictates that nobility fight on horseback; I hope that is not an issue."

"I came of age in Edward's court. Horseback is fine."

"But you prefer to fight on foot."

"Of course. An Englishman with a Dane axe is worth a man and a horse in any fight."

"You will see how times have changed."

"If every man fought on donkeys, the field would change the same," Harold laughs, and watches the knights and men-at-arms move on ahead, banners fluttering in the slight breeze under a wan sky.

*   *   *

The weather threatens but never breaks as the French and their English invitees leave the orchards and marshes of Dol-de-Bretagne and traipse towards Brittany's nascent shoots of wheat and grain. Their target is Dinan if they cannot goad Conan into a fight by firing up the countryside. They begin to organize the crossing of the river Cousenon, at a place their horses can ford. Things progress apace, the marshes sucking at the horses' hooves. Men shed their armour to lighten the load as the horses up front start to sink to their knees. Then a flock of arrows rains down upon them.

"Aux Arms!" The cry goes up. Men and horses panic under fire and a few are thrown from their horses into the boggy ground. Turning, Harold spots two men under fire struggling to extricate themselves from the bog. He yells to his men to dismount and raise their shields, and jumps from his own destrier, holding his own shield above his head as arrows thud and splash around them. A group of lightly armoured men race ahead on ponies and loose their own arrows wildly at the unseen enemy. Harold forces his way across to two of the downed men, and reaching down with his right arms hauls one onto his back in one big sweep, holding his shield the whole time. The other is beginning to sink, so he grabs him under his armpit and hauls. Around him, the arrows stop and men begin to calm as he wrenches the man from the hungry bog and drags him behind all the way across the river ford. Then he dumps the grateful pair on the far side, shrugging the one off like a sack of wheat and returns to fetch another. Off to his left a man is drowning and the armoured knights cannot get to him.

"Too late," he says, and reaches for another, dragging the wretch out. Order is restored among the French as Odo rides among them barking orders. He beams at Harold.

"Harold! You are one of a kind—what earl would save these men at risk of his own skin?"

"Sicut Sanctus Christophorus fecit, ita sequor."

This is reported to William who rides up to greet Harold.

"Well done," he says in his best broken English and gives Harold a rare smile.

"Now I need to find my shoes," the earl laughs.

After the ambush, the French mood towards the Bretons changes. Few are spared on the short march onwards, though the destruction is not great. Peasant women are passed among the men so often many die from the constant assault, and those Breton men not killed watch as their daughters and wives are stripped in front of them. Conan organizes a few ambushes, and word travels that he is assembled south of the French forces near the marshes of the Rance valley. William agrees to a detour and sends a detachment to watch Dinan as his forces move towards their prey. The ground is tacky underfoot and beautiful in spring. Harold spurs his horse to William and Odo.

"This is perfect ground for an ambush."

"Yes, like your Welsh campaign, we are hoping for some such thing. Any fight to bring the man to heel," Odo smiles at Harold. "You see how well our minds work together, brother."

Half a day in they get word that Conan has moved again. William says a harsh word to Odo, who smarts at his brother's ill temper. But they go on, skirting the marshes, as French soldiers smile and wave to Harold, word spreading of the hero Englishman who treats the common man as an equal.

Conan's attempt to lead them on a merry chase through Northern Brittany, with its mix of fertile fields and marshes and a tongue so close to Welsh, Wulfric can converse with many of the men and women spared the Norman lash ends quickly. It is Wulfric, who tells Harold, who tells Odo, that Conan is holed up in Dinan so the army turns in one great pivot and heads back to their original target. The watching party manages to halt a sally by Conan, who is back in his tower within moments of attempting to break free. On a granite cliff face, with a guarded river crossing, the keep, as the French call it, is perfectly.

"Care to sneak up and take the fort at night," Odo suggests. William seems pleased at the camaraderie between his brother and the most powerful man in England.

"I have three of my best men and two of the bravest Thegns in England. Why not? We'll need a rope ladder...." Harold reels off a long list of equipment and ends with the need for a support army, just in case. Odo grins at him and orders an encirclement of the fort, organizing gangs of soldiers to clear the area to the South and West of the "castle" before settling an army above and around the keep.

"Now what," asks Harold. Ulfwith and Wiglaf are eager for a fight and offer themselves up to assault the walls.

"No no," the Bishop says. "We have encircled. Now we wait."

"We wait."

"Yes. We lay siege to the castle, we ravage around the grounds and we starve the bastard out."

And so they wait, sending volleys of arrows into the town and harassing the inhabitants around Dinan. Conan can only watch as his people are raped and beaten in front of his walls. Rumours begin to circulate that Harold Godwinson has come to take his head at night and a white flag goes up at the main gate. The Elderly Roger is sent with a few knights to the gate where terms are set. After a day of preparations, the gates open and a magnificent Conan rides out alone, spurring his horse to a canter with his spear in the upright position. He rides straight towards William, whose men shout in alarm. William rides up on his own horse, sword drawn, to meet Conan. Conan continues, lowering his spear to the attack position, his mail and helmet glinting under a bright morning sun. Then he stops suddenly. On the tip of the spear is a key.

"He is giving his castle to the Duke," says Hereward.

"That's it?"

"It appears so, lord."

After Conan, a group of knights sally out. They dismount and offer their swords up in a kneeling position. Then the women are led on palfreys to William's nods and greetings. Conan will forfeit his garrison, and pay a fine, but keep Dinan so long as William's own garrison is stationed there. His knights are each to pay a fine and pledge allegiance on sacred relics to William alone. Then the troops are marched out. They lay down their arms and stand in formation. At William's command, the men are forced to kneel and bound. They are put into three groups. The first group are bound to posts. A group of soldiers are set about putting hot pokers into a fire, then another group approach these men and begin to gouge their eyes out. The English watch in horror. The screams of these men drown out the heckling of the French forces. The hot pokers staunch the bleeding, and the men are left tied to their stakes.

The next group have a hand cut off. In an act of charity, Harold is led to understand, it is the left hand only. Their stubs have a hot iron applied. By now the screams are all they can hear and even the French soldiers are quiet. The next group have a foot amputated. One man who screams abuse at the French forces has both feet and a hand. He passes out from the pain. The final group, who seem relieved at being spared the amputations are stripped of their clothes and forced out into the countryside. To return is death.

"Lord protect us," Harold utters.

"To kill these men is to deny them a chance of absolution," Odo says mildly, "disabled thus, they may be penitents, under the care of the Church."

"And Conan is simply fined."

"Yes, and brought back into the fold of William's just clemency."

"Such things divide us, Odo."

"Then we must seek to close that gap." A horde of monks are sent to take the garrison into their care.

"Alors," William rides over "fait accompli." FitzOsbern makes bear hands at Harold and growls. Even William smiles at this.

"The Duke thanks you for the…intelligence, and your bravery has not gone unnoticed Duke Harold," says Jean.

"We didn't even get a fucking skirmish," Algar moans.

"Just a visit to the butcher's," says Ulfwith. "I want to go home. Let's go fight the Scots, Harold."

"Now, Odo," Harold says. "My brother."

Odo raises his hand. "Of course. He will be waiting for you. But before we go, Guillaume has something for you."

William motions for Harold to come to him and flicks a finger at a group of servants. They bring a set of exquisite mail to him, along with a helmet embossed with gold.

"Pour moi?"

"Oui."

"Merci Guillaume. In return—translate this—I give you a goshawk that survived our storm and is my favourite bird of prey. Perhaps we shall go hunting together." Odo nods appreciatively.

"Est-ce que tu acceptes?" William seems impatient.

"Oui, J'accepte."

"Bon." And William gives the rarest of smiles.

*   *   *

Wulfnoth doesn't rise when Harold enters the bright courtyard. Their eyes meet for a second before Harold looks away.

"You look…well…brother," Wulfnoth says. He has grown into a tall man, like his brothers, but his voice is hollow, and inflected with French, much like Edward's.

"It has been…a long time Wulfnoth. When you were taken, we were, all of us, in a panic or rage."

"Did you hit Swein for what he did to all of us?"

"I knocked the bastard to the ground."

"To think…of all of us…his soul will go to heaven."

"It is the strangest of—ironies as the French would say."

"Yes…ironies."

"Brother—"

"Don't Harold."

"I failed you."

"Yes. Father did too. If you came looking for absolution, look elsewhere." He is a Godwin, yet not—not broken but holding himself with the emptiness of a man orphaned by his family's neglect.

"Can you stand?"

"Yes, of course. They…treat me well. I have a house, a French wife."

"Children?"

"No. God has not blessed me."

"I have—"

"Yes, a brood. And Wyn?"

"Wyn is the finest of us all. He would be here—would have come earlier, much earlier…but I cannot risk another brother."

"We were close—the four of us, with Gyrth."

"Brother." Harold kneels, his face ashen.

"Don't Harold. I told you."

"These long years I have fought for the stability our father never left us. That chance of exile despite our power. And now the King and I are one on most matters, I finally have what I sought. But what is it without my…"

"Without your duty to your family."

"Yes."

"It is power, Harold. Power and strength."

Wulfnoth's eyes are blank and he looks around distractedly. Harold turns away for a moment and rises again.

"You know, I always thought of becoming a priest."

"There are many tell me that would have been good for our family."

"Bishop Wulfnoth."

"I like it."

"Why now, Harold?"

"The opportunity arose. I want my family whole."

"But why? I'm the youngest brother. You have three others. Is this for pride?"

"You mean having a brother as a hostage?"

"Yes."

"Nobody would expect me to invade Normandy."

"Swein's son Hakon is here too. He is…"

"Like a nephew to you?"

"A good…boy, more a man now."

"And I should see this son of Swein? He was just a baby when he was taken."

"The cause of Swein's redemption."

"Walking somewhere doesn't change your soul. I have often asked Odo about you."

"And yet here I stayed all these years until I finally gave up."

"I am here now." Wulfnoth shrugs. "You are still young, younger than Wyn. You have a chance to be what you will." His brother shakes his head and bites his lower lip.

"William is…a hard man, Harold. He will not trade me for anything other than a halter around your neck."

"He might for something else."

"What shall I do in England? Potter around and go hunting?"

"It's what Edward does." It draws a thin smile.

"So, you are king in all but name."

"No, I am the Earl of Wessex, and you are my brother."

"Do what you will Harold. Now, I left my psalter somewhere here." He looks around again.

"Brother—"

"I am fine, Harold. It would be good to see the others."

"Yes."

Harold moves to grasp his brother's shoulder but stops as Wulfnoth flinches. He nods and turns towards the doorway. As he closes the door he presses his fist into his mouth. Then he draws a deep breath and lets it out through pursed lips.

*   *   *

The next day he wakes in a merchant's requisitioned house in Dol-de-Bretagne, a little life having left him. His servant comes in and begins his grooming, setting aside the clothes for the day. The room is hung with simple tapestries sewn with scenes of trade and ships, and the walls are painted a deep blue. The furniture is so heavy it is as if they built the house around the bed and tables. Harold spent the morning lifting and lowering the bed above his men's quarters. Their curses and stomping around made him smile again.

"I'll be talking with William today about my brother."

"Yes my lord," the servant, Arnulf, says. He is Danish, thin and middling height, with a wispy moustache and pronounced cheekbones.

"Arnulf."

"Yes lord."

"Do you miss home?"

"I was poor at home and less poor here. But I miss my mother."

"When I was exiled, all I thought of was getting back. Taking my Earldom back."

"We common folk have no earldoms to take or take back lord, just our bellies to feed and our masters to please."

"You are a free man, though."

"Of course, Earl Harold."

After his grooming, he dresses, straps on his axe and sword and leaves his room in the merchant's vast house. Breakfast is being made for the earl by one of William's cooks. The whole town has been requisitioned for the nobility, and there is barely a murmur from the townspeople. He sits down to his meal of pheasant, bacon, eggs and bread with his men, who now sit in order of rank, down the table from him.

"Well boys. That was quite the adventure."

"Not a single fucking fight," Ulfwith remarks, yawning and still sore at Harold.

"Just a visit to the butchers," Hereward notes bitterly.

"That has not been done in England since Cnut, and never at that scale," Wulfric says.

"Of all the men I have slain, I cannot remember doing such an act, even in the rage of battle."

"And the lords get off with a weregild and a slap," says Olaf.

"It is a brutal way to be sure," says Harold.

"And yet how they treat the women—like the Virgin Mary came down from heaven and gave them a wink," Hereward shakes his head.

"Now that is worthy of a finger at least," Ulfwith laughs. Algar is silent; he has been withdrawn since the scene outside Dinan.

"We shall be home soon, Algar," says Harold. "Not to worry—I haven't picked up any ideas, save their castles. Now those could come in useful at the Scottish border."

"A perfect stye to pen you up in lord, while they ravage the country around you."

"Perhaps, Hereward."

"I am done with this place, lord," says Olaf shaking his large head. "But the food is good."

"It really is good. You know, that's a thing about Edward—his cooks are really the best."

"Edward the King?"

"Yes."

"The best thing about him is his cooking?"

"No, that's not what I said."

"Word will get around of this treason," Algar finally speaks, and the men burst out laughing.

*　　*　　*

They exit their quarters armed and ready to talk with William. Outside the streets are festive. People of all ranks dressed gaily. Jean, dressed in a fine "livery", newly knighted it seems by William or Odo, approaches the men with a big smile.

"Gentlemen, Earl Harold, good morning! Duke William and Bishop Odo would like to speak with you."

"That is good news, as I have need to speak with them."

"Alors, come with me if you please."

They mount their horses to avoid walking in the filth of the streets. The clop through the town, soldiers and townsfolk alike making way in natural obeisance, through the market square and out through the stone gate of the town. There, the air is foul around the walls and ditch, but a hundred steps ahead the breeze picks up and they smell the freshness of the countryside. All around them the sound of men laughing and joking, servants in bright clothes running through the fields, setting up tents and carrying meat for a feast. Ahead is a large canopy, where they make out the figures of Harold and Odo, and sundry priests around them.

The Englishmen dismount.

"Bonjour Guillaume."

"Bonjour, Arold. Commen vas-tu?"

"Bon, et Vu?"

"Tres bon, mon ami."

"Frater!" Odo gives great hug to the big man, surprised again at Harold's breadth and vigour.

In Latin—"I seek my brother and nephew's release."

"Yes," says Odo mildly, "but first we must talk."

"It was Robert of Jumièges who took him, and now there is no conflict between our families, there should be no need for retaining him in your custody."

William observes the exchange blankly. Odo turns his head and rapidly translates; William rolls his eyes and motions for Odo to continue. Odo gives Harold that tolerant smile of the dutiful brother; the same smile that Wyn gives.

"It is important to my brother that you agree to uphold his rights and do him no harm. In exchange, he will return your—relative."

"We are here by accident, what need does he have of my assurances."

"Your people have a strong navy and are beginning to look outwards, as Cnut did. It is important we do not come into conflict as our nations…grow."

"So you are worried two bears may tread on each other's turf."

"Exactly this—and also that we follow your king's will in all things."

"The succession is the King's choice, and the Witan's decision. You know this, Odo."

"Yes—my brother still needs an…education…in such matters but I understand your ways."

"No man can take the throne in England and expect the people will lie down and take it."

"Our ways are different, yes. Swear an oath, Harold, to respect his rights and be done with it."

"To respect his rights."

"Yes."

William nods to Harold. "Mes droits."

Before the Earl are three priests, a table adorned with an altar cloth, with a large gilt-bound Bible on top of it. William stands two paces to the left, his men arranged in rank beside him. There is another table, decked in a finer altar cloth. The gathered host, obviously rushed, are attempting solemnity.

"What is this, Harold," Ulfwith asks.

"Some French trick," mutters Wulfstan.

"Well then," says Harold, "Let's see what we can do about this."

"Take care of your soul, Lord," Hereward says, out of character.

"It's not my soul I'm worried about." To Odo: "His rights?"

"Yes, brother." Odo smiles sympathetically, as Harold suppresses a half smile.

*   *   *

Harold strides into the King's solar with a young man of similar appearance behind him, along with his thegns and Housecarls. Surrounded by bright French tapestries of hunting and saintly miracles, the servants tactful furniture beside the walls, Leofwyn and Gyrth sit together expectantly. Tostig is reading from a psalter. The king is absent, but the great lords stir at the coming of the earl.

"What news, Harold?" Gyrth is up out of his chair.

"We were blown off course and held hostage by some French pirate. Duke William bailed us out."

The Oath, 1064

"Who's this then," Leofwyn gestures at the boy.

"Hakon."

"Swein's son, Hakon?"

Harold nods. The youth is looking around the room nervously.

"Where's Wulfstan, then?" The earl shakes his head and looks away.

"Speak English," Leofwyn asks and the youth nods.

"Hopefully you're not like your father, boy."

"You call him boy," Tostig laughs.

"I'm an earl now," he grins.

"What's this William like?" Leofwyn is still grinning at the youth.

"A total cunt."

All the men sit up, the blunt force statement rousing them further.

"I hear you campaigned with William." Harold nods. "How is their warfare next to ours?"

"They spend their time building these…castles, that they hide in and besiege and nobody seems to do any fighting. They just march around setting fire to villages and surrounding towns until they starve the enemy out."

"Sounds like us in Wales. What then?"

"They spare the lords and cut the hands and feet off of their men."

"And gouge out their eyes," Ulfwith pipes up.

"Give me a drink would you," he motions to a servant.

"The soldiers?"

"Yes, and the lords go on their way."

"Come now," Ralph the king's nephew stammered, his bony frame shaking slightly at speaking. "This is something of an exaggeration."

"I saw it with my own eyes," Harold looks around the hall.

"This will never stand in England," Stigand for once seems morally outraged. "What outrage is this?"

Harold motions for Hakon to greet his uncles; Gyrth and Leofwyn rise as he attempts awkward handshakes and grasp him in a double bear hug. He gasps as they force him down on a chair and look him over.

"I have heard of this," says Edwin. Tostig cocks an eyebrow at him.

"It's good for the lords, sounds like we can do what we want and get away with it." Gyrth laughs but the room is silent.

"He cannot be king," Bishop Wulfstan says flatly.

"Who then?"

Harold nods over to Edgar, sitting wide eyed at the scene.

"That boy?" Gyrth shakes his head.

"Yes, that boy."

"I think Harold should be king," Leofwyn says, equally flatly.

"Don't," replies Harold.

"Good thing Edward isn't here," laughs Tostig. Harold shakes his head.

"And why are you here," Stigand asks the Northern earl. "Half of Northumbria is up in arms."

"Half of Northumbria is always up in arms," says Tostig; Edwin looks shocked. "Besides, my men have their orders. I shall return soon. What else, brother?"

"He made me swear an oath."

"An oath?"

"Yes, an oath." By now Harold is moving to a chair and slumps in it.

"What kind of an oath."

"A most sacred and holy one by the sound of it," Gyrth laughs.

"He made me put my hand on a cloth, and swear to support his rights, or Wulfstan would be…placed outside of his protection."

"That cunt."

"Exactly that."

"Except the cloth lord…" Olaf prompts.

"The cloth. The cloth covered some relics." The duke had smiled that blank smile and motioned his priest to show the relics underneath. Harold breathes deeply at the childish trick. There is silence in the close room.

"The heresy!" Stigand shouts.

Harold shakes his head. "I swore to uphold his rights, not his fucking claim: relax. The Witan confirms a king."

"Brother an oath given under duress or through trickery is not binding in god's name, anyway." Tostig was standing straight now. "We cannot allow this man to be king."

"He cannot be king." Wulfstan repeats.

"Edward will name his successor and the Witan will confirm it, let's keep our heads."

Ralph had risen at the same time as Harold sat and begins to head out of the main doors. Stigand rolls his eyes as he rushes out.

"What else, Harold?"

"Duke William did give our lord some fine armour," Olaf pipes up from his place by the door.

"Armor?" Olaf nodded.

"That means he's your liege now," Wulfstan says.

"What," says Harold.

"My lord was brave in an ambush and rescued men from quicksand – it was a gift."

"Brother." Leofwyn says flatly and rises to place his hand on Harold's shoulder.

"Is this true," Harold seems alarmed.

"Accepting a gift of armour is a sign of "homage" as these French call it."

"How did I not know this?" Hereward shrugs and looks away.

"Brother," Leofwyn says dolefully, shaking his head.

Just then the king walks in, sister Edith and servants in dutiful tow.

"Harold! Welcome. What news of France?"

"Duke William gave Harold some armour." says Gyrth, placing his hand upon his brother's shoulder.

"Oh, you're his man now, Harold." Harold tips his head back as the king smiles.

"You were my hero, brother. Now…" Harold sweeps his hand off and stands. "Now you're just a Norman pup." Gyrth bellows with laughter. Even Tostig laughs. "Did he also… touch you in special places?"

"Stop! Stop," laughs the king.

Leofwyn begins to leave.

"Where are you going," Gyrth asks.

"To find a new hero. Perhaps to France to meet this William." Leofwyn grins and leaves the hall laughing.

"So not the best visit then, Harold," the king says. "Perhaps next time you should tell me where you're going so I can…assist?"

"We were blown off course, Edward."

"God has a funny way of testing us for sure, Harold. Now come, let us talk together. I felt an ache this morning. Perhaps it is time."

About the Author

G.R Coldicott is a writer of historical fiction. Drawing on meticulous research, he brings to life the political intrigue, military campaigns, and personal rivalries that shaped England before the Norman Conquest. The Oath is the first book of The Godwinson Quartet series.

In the Next Book: *The Bridge*

The story of Godwin, Beorn, and Swein, Tostig's struggles in the North, and the fratricidal rifts that tear England apart.